The Only Way …………and More.

A collection of short stories

By Gina Thompson

Acknowledgements

This is different to my previous novels – it is a collection of five novelettes for those of us that haven't the time - or the patience – to read a full-length novel.

I began with the intention of writing short stories for magazines but found it very difficult to be succinct enough, as my friends all know that I cannot just give plain facts when I am relating anything – I need to 'go round the houses ' to get where I want to be! I also had in mind the idea that a collection of short stories might make useful holiday reading, so I set about it with that purpose in mind.

However, from the beginning of 2020 we watched in trepidation as the Corona virus, Covid 19, swept across the world and then from March our country also went into lockdown. I was fortunate in the fact that I lived next door to my family and therefore we were classed as sharing a household and consequently I did not have to make the sacrifices that almost everyone else had to make by not being able to see their loved ones. It was hard taking on the task of home-schooling three children aged five, seven and nine years old, but my family have always supported me so this was my opportunity to support my daughter, Kelly, who works for the NHS and my son-in-law, Richard, who both worked full-time during this period as key workers.

I wanted to show the children that I too was doing my own version of 'schoolwork' by writing on an evening. This had the advantage of opening up an avenue of discussion with my granddaughters who liked to help me think up ideas for storylines on the walk to school when the school re-opened in mid-June and who offered suggestions that I gratefully accepted, so thank you Arabella and Alexa, my beautiful princesses! I should also mention my grandson, Joshua, who at that time wasn't really interested in anything that didn't have superpowers, but he is my own little superhero!

I am blessed to have some wonderful, loyal friends who encourage me to write and do not criticise but simply accept that I write for pleasure and nothing else. Those who are particularly supportive are 'the Pellon ladies' in Halifax – Nancy, Tanya, Margaret, Florrie, Lyn, Gwen and Rachel. Among my Keighley friends giving me the same level of encouragement are Liz, Carmel, Rachel and Pauline and I am grateful to them all for their tireless allegiance.

I owe a debt of gratitude to Janice, currently living in Stoke-on-Trent caring for her mum and who encouraged me to write a novel in the first instance and who continues to be my advisor for legal facts that may arise in any of my stories.

I hope you enjoy these stories – they are all fiction, but those who know me may detect in some of them very slight hints of real-life events that I may have shared with them over the years!

Thank you all.

Gina.

Table of contents

Contents

The Only Way.

"Here we are, girls," said the taxi driver as they pulled up outside driveway of the double-fronted detached house at the end of the quiet cul-de-sac.

"Thank you, my good man," slurred a female voice, "Take care of my friend, make sure she gets home safely!" she hiccupped, "Goodnight, sweetie, I'll see you on Monday!" Tina lurched out of the car door and blowing kisses to the other occupant who was slumped in the corner of the seat and receiving a floppy wave in return, she staggered up the gravelled drive to her front door. She eventually managed to get her key into the lock and slowly opened the door.

"Shhh!" she said to no-one in particular and putting her finger to her lips in an exaggerated movement she said again, "Shhhh!" while looking around. The hall light was still on – the rule was that the last one in turned the lights off. That posed a problem – was Ben home or not? She couldn't remember - had he gone out tonight or did he stay home – again – fiddling about on the computer doing………..whatever he did? "Boring! Boring Ben!" she pouted, then giggled at what she perceived as funny.

She went into the kitchen and sat down heavily on the chair near the large kitchen table. "A nightcap! That's what I need!" She stood up, scraping the chair backwards as she tottered to the wine rack in the corner and pulled out a bottle without looking at it then snatched a wineglass as she staggered her way back to the table. She missed the chair as she went to sit down and crashed heavily to the floor landing on her backside still clutching the wineglass and bottle. She began to giggle as she looked from one hand to the other. "Didn't drop the wine, did you? Well done! Good work, girl!"

The door opened and a face appeared slowly, a deep frown etched across his brow. As he rounded the door, Ben said, "What on earth are you doing? Did you fall?"

"Missed the chair – but saved the wine!" Tina laughed idiotically, "Help me up, I need a drink."

"I think you've had more than enough!" said Ben, irritation hollowing his voice but he bent towards her and grasping her by the elbows, he hauled her to her feet.

"Don't be boring!" she slurred, "Boring Ben! Have a drink with me!"

"No, thank you!" he snapped, "I'm going back to bed! That's where I think you should go!" He turned to go out but she grabbed his arm.

"Why won't you have a drink with me?" she demanded, "You're not fun any more! When did you become this ………..boring, Ben?"

He looked at her with a mixture of contempt and pity, then shook his head hopelessly. "I can't even talk to you when you're like this," he said sadly and with slumped shoulders he went out of the kitchen.

Tina banged the bottle and the glass on the table and lurched out of the door after him. "You've spoilt it now! I'd had a good night – just one more drink…….a little nightcap, that's all I wanted, but you've spoilt it now!"

She attempted to climb the stairs behind him but struggled to keep upright, so she crawled on her hands and knees. When she reached the bedroom, she pulled herself upright but was then flung back against the wall as Ben barged out of the room carrying his pillow from their bed. She looked at him, blinking and widening her eyes as she tried to focus, but then with an exaggerated sigh, she turned and went into the bedroom, slamming the door behind her.

"Fine!" she shouted, "Sleep in the spare room! See if I care!" She wrenched off her jacket and vainly tried to reach the zipper on the back of her dress but gave up with a petulant whimper. She kicked off her shoes and climbed into bed fully clothed, her whimpering becoming louder and turning into angry exclamations of annoyance. However, after ten minutes or so, she was asleep, her jaw hanging slackly and slight snores coming from her open mouth.

In the guest bedroom next door, Ben could hear the noises coming from the marital bedroom so he knew she was in bed and asleep. He quietly crept out of bed and opened the bedroom door slowly and carefully – although he knew from past experience a mighty crash of thunder wouldn't wake her once she was asleep after drinking so much. He carefully crept past her door and went downstairs.

When did it get like this? He asked himself this same question every time his wife came in drunk like this or when he came home and found her in a similar state, usually passed out on the sofa. With a furrowed brow he shook his head slowly and sorrowfully. *It all began when she started the new job and got in with that party crowd!* he admitted silently to himself. *She's not the same person - she rarely sees any of her old friends anymore, but I doubt they'd want to know her now the way she is.*

With a deep sigh he boiled the kettle and made a cup of tea. He carried it into the lounge and turned on the television, flicking through the channels till he found something that wasn't a shopping channel – he couldn't bear to look at a shopping channel since Tina got the job working at one in the

TV studio! He could see through the 'genuineness' of the presenters, he now had an insight into the hedonistic lifestyles that were at the back of the unrelenting salespeople. He finally came across an old black and white movie that he settled back to watch, but he couldn't focus on it – his mind went back over the scene he had encountered in the kitchen and he asked himself the same question he asked every time this happened. What could he do to change things? How could he stop her from getting drunk like this regularly? How could he stop her from going out with this crowd of people without becoming a controlling husband. He gave a scornful splutter. *As if she could ever be controlled! SHE'S the dominant one!* He laughed sardonically. *No, me becoming bossy and forceful will have the opposite effect………..I just don't know how to handle the situation………..guess I'll just have to hope she grows out of it – before it's too late, because I don't know how much more of this I can take!*

He drained his tea and brought his attention back to the television, but then realised that the film had finished and a new programme had started – an old western movie with lots of cattle stampeding and cowboys trying to restrain them. He turned off the television and after turning off all the lights and taking his cup into the kitchen he made his way upstairs. He paused outside the bedroom door and he could hear her gentle snoring, intercepted by some unintelligible ramblings, but he was satisfied that she was asleep – and still alive! That was his main fear – that she would choke on her own vomit! That's what had happened to his father's best friend many years ago and he remembered how it had affected the man's family, but also how it had affected his father! He never saw his father inebriated after that – and when Ben was a teenager going through his rebellious stage and was carried home one night by his friends and deposited on the doorstep, completely comatose after drinking almost a full bottle of vodka – he saw his father cry. His father was a giant of a man, rarely showing affection to his children as he was of the generation that thought showing feelings meant showing weakness, so when Ben woke up and his father was hunched over his bed, holding his hand and weeping brokenly, it was burned into his memory. He was so ill for three days afterwards he never wanted to repeat the ordeal nor did he want to be responsible for his father's tears ever again.

The following morning he was downstairs reading the newspaper when Tina came into the kitchen. He'd already been to the gym – he always did an early Saturday morning workout and was waiting for Tina to come down so they could have breakfast together, and he looked up with some trepidation as she came in. She'd been in the shower and was wrapped in her bathrobe with a towelling turban round her head and she grimaced sheepishly as she pulled out a chair across from Ben at the table.

"Sorry about last night – I think I was a bit ………err…….worse for wear!" she said.

Ben sighed. "I don't want to start a row with you and I don't want to sound as if I'm nagging…….but I do worry about how much you're drinking – it's getting worse."

He saw the flash of annoyance cross her face and he inwardly steeled himself against her temper flare-up. "Just don't, Ben, just don't! I enjoy going out with my friends and yes, we DO drink ……….too much by your standards I know, but we just have fun, we're not hurting anybody!"

"Except yourselves!" he countered, "Don't you realise the damage that you're doing to your body when you drink to excess on a regular basis? If you would only come to the gym with me……….a good workout would help to flush the toxins out of your body……"

"I've told you before, Ben, I'm not interested in going to the gym! That's something YOU enjoy, so crack on with it…….just leave me to live my own life the way I want to! I don't expect you to come drinking and dancing with me – don't expect me to go to the gym with you!" She got up from the chair and walked over to the fridge. She took out a carton of orange juice and poured herself a glass.

"I'll do some breakfast for us, then I'm going shopping. Do you want to come…….." she asked watching him through narrowed eyes as she gulped down the orange juice.

"I've got some stuff I need to be getting on with if that's okay……….unless you need me to come to carry bags?" he said, hoping she would refuse – he hated shopping.

"No, I'm only doing a supermarket shop, we've run out of a lot of things – I can manage." She started to get the things out of the fridge to do a full English breakfast which was their weekend treat as weekdays usually meant a snatched cereal bar or hastily toasted slice of bread while the kettle boiled.

He busied himself making the toast and the coffee while she grilled the bacon and sausage and fried the eggs, tomatoes and mushrooms, then they sat quietly enjoying their Saturday breakfast. He had turned his attention back to the newspaper and was reading the sport page when Tina suddenly said musingly, "Do you realise that in three years we will be in the next century?"

Ben looked up. "I know, even though there's lots of stuff around about 'preparing for the millennium', saying that

we're going into the 'next century' seems much more…………
dramatic somehow!"

"So in the year 2000 we will have been married ten years and we will both be thirty-five years old! We'll be forty in the year 2005! Do we say 'two thousand and five, or twenty oh-five?" she pondered, holding her coffee cup next to her cheek.

"I think we can please ourselves," he replied, "Whichever you're most comfortable with." Ben was happy just to be having a normal Saturday morning conversation when so many in the past had been full of accusations and acrimony. He felt himself mellow towards her – again – and he felt a flicker of hope take hold inside him. "Do you want me to come supermarket shopping with you? I can do what I need to do later."

"If you want," she said standing up, "It's up to you. I said I'd meet Sarah in the coffee shop afterwards – but you're welcome to tag along." She started to clear the table, but he said, "I'll do that – you go and get dressed. I'll just stay home today."

He felt the little candle-flame of hope extinguish with a splutter. Her drinking buddies still took priority – even on weekend days when traditionally this was supposed to be family time. Except they had no family – well, no children!

She'd said many times that she wasn't ready for them – his siblings had their own lives, his father had passed away and his mum was in a nursing home and any family get-togethers only happened on very special occasions. He felt a gulf of loneliness widen before him and pulled himself up sharply. She may still come back to the girl he knew and loved, not this party animal who seemed only interested in having a good time with her friends.

As he loaded the dishwasher and wiped down the kitchen benches, he thought back over their life together. They were sweethearts from being fifteen years old, in the same class at school then went to the same college - he did business studies and she did marketing and publicity and they qualified at the same time after three years. All the time they were at college, they did everything together. Neither of them drank much – he would have a cider and blackcurrant and she would have a lager with lime, but this was mainly for show and rarely did they have a second drink when they were out with friends. They were obviously very much in love and their college friends classed them as one unit – in fact they were often referred to as 'Bentina'! They still had fun, lots of it, and their three years in college passed very quickly.

In Tina's first job she was made redundant after two and a half years due to the company streamlining the department, but within a couple of months she had secured a place in the company that she currently worked for. Tina was coming up to twenty-five – Ben had already had his twenty-fifth birthday - when they got married. They had bought a small terraced house the year after she got this new job and saved for a further two years so she could have the wedding she dreamed of. It was at this job where she first began to go for nights out without Ben, but as most of the staff team was female it had always been a girls' night out where the partners of those who were in a relationship didn't get invited. They danced and laughed and always asked the DJ to play 'Girls just wanna have fun," which they claimed as 'their song'.

Ben didn't worry too much about it at first as he had enrolled at college to do a photography course on an evening, and when Tina's nights out increased, he increased his own outside interests and joined a gym. He began to worry when she started to come home drunk and he voiced his concern, mainly about her safety and the impact on her health, but after weeks and months of it happening, it always ended up in a bitter row and nothing ever changed. She resented what she saw as him trying to control her, and he resented the fact that she was blatantly disregarding his past distress connected to his father's friend dying through alcohol abuse and his father's tears at Ben getting drunk as a teenager and the impact this had had on Ben throughout his life.

So, he stopped saying anything to her and tried to be in bed when she came home and if he was woken as he was on Friday night, he would go and sleep in the spare room. That had been the pattern for the past four or five years and had only got worse over this period of time – she had started to drink a bottle of wine on the nights when she stayed home. He didn't know what to do about it. He was relieved his father wasn't alive to see how much she drank and his mum was now in a nursing home after developing Alzheimer's and on the occasions that Tina went with him to visit, it was daytime and she was sober so no-one suspected anything. Her own parents weren't bothered by her drinking as they themselves enjoyed a few drinks in the pub a couple of times a week. Nobody guessed the extent of her alcohol misuse, and Ben had nobody he could talk to about it so he kept it to himself and it lay like a stone in his stomach.

His mind was brought back to the present when he heard her come down the stairs. She was dressed to go out and she came into the kitchen to check the fridge for items that they would need. Neither of them spoke except to say ''Bye' and as she went out of the door he called to her, "Will you be home for dinner?"

She stopped in her tracks and whirled round, "Are you making a joke?" she asked uncertainly.

"I'm simply asking if you'll be home for dinner tonight," he said.

"I'm going shopping at the supermarket! Of course I'll be home for dinner! In fact, I'll bring something nice and we can have a special meal to show I'm sorry about being a boozy, frivolous wife!" She was using her puppy-dog expression to win him round – which always used to work, but lately he felt a flash of annoyance when she did this. It had ceased to be appealing to him and he turned away before his expression gave it away.

He felt her hand on his arm and he turned to face her. She leaned into him and nestled into his chest. His arms instinctively went round her and her arms clasped round his waist. He kissed the top of her head, inhaling the scent of her freshly washed hair and murmured, "I'm sorry I'm such a nag, but I worry about what it's doing to your health!"

"I know," she purred.

He released his arms and she picked up her bag and blowing him a kiss she went out of the door. He took a deep breath in and exhaled loudly. Why couldn't he be more dynamic – he knew she would continue this pattern of behaviour, but all he could do was hope that it would eventually pass. He'd first excused her by saying she'd missed out on this kind of rebellious behaviour when she was a teenager because they were a couple from being fifteen years old and he had never wanted to do the heavy drinking and boisterous teen antics because of what happened with his father, so he had accepted that perhaps she *needed* to go through it in her adult life. But she hadn't come out the other side – and this heavy drinking had gone on for over four years and Ben was becoming more and more unhappy.

He went out through the kitchen door and down to the summerhouse. It was a beautiful building, created on the lines of a Scandinavian log cabin with a patio and was separated from the house by a paved path with lawns on either side. The garden was easy to maintain and the summerhouse was something that they'd both wanted almost as soon as they moved into the house and had spent many nights designing and planning it, but eventually handed their ideas to a professional who had produced this wonderful creation.

Ben unlocked the door and pinned it back to get fresh air into the room. It was a warm, muggy morning and promised to be a scorcher my mid-afternoon. On the back wall was a unit with a television and video player on one side and a CD player on the other. The cabinet at the front housed the CDs and videos and the other two cabinets stored the vast collection of photographs that he had accumulated over their years together. He took out the box of photographs from his college course of the various projects that he had undertaken and browsed through them. He had filed them chronologically so he could track his development in skill and artistry as he progressed through the course and felt a surge of pleasure and satisfaction as he acknowledged his accomplishment. The final section in this box held his 'field trip' photos – when he went out for a ramble he always took a camera and photographed various subjects that he found appealing to his artists eye. He mentally noted that he would need another box as this one was tightly packed now.

He took out another small box of photographs which was divided into sections, similar to a filing cabinet, where every section was labelled with whatever was contained in it. This box housed all the photos of his early years and childhood - photos of his parents and extended family and all of his life before he met Tina. Many of these photographs were in black and white because the cost of colour film development was much more expensive then. The next box he took out was a record of their life together. It was much larger in length and was also divided and labelled according to the years they represented – some sections holding more photographs than others when there were more things happening. For instance there were lots of photographs in the year they had the summerhouse built showing its development, then the before-and-after photographs of the garden when they had it landscaped, then the year they went on their first cruise. Every year had holiday photographs as well as other things that had happened and as he browsed he noticed how materialistic their lives had gradually become.

He went back to the first couple of sections which began when they were both fifteen. There weren't many photographs in the first year – most were poor quality by current standards and had been taken with a small Kodak camera, which, from 1989 onwards progressed to sharper focus from the Konica camera that they used for many years until Ben took up photography seriously and he invested in a couple of good quality cameras, which he had upgraded several times over the years. However, the first few photos showed a young teenage couple, laughing up at each other, both wearing shell-suits and curly hair. Later years saw them dressed in denim jeans and jackets but their activities were still concentrated on each other's presence and the simple things in life, whereas later sections showed possessions and signs of a much more comfortable lifestyle.

Then his attention was taken by the largest section - 1990, the year they got married. They had lived together for two years before they married and he remembered with an aching heart how wonderful their life had been then. On their wedding day he recalled how stunning she had looked as she walked down the aisle towards him and how nervous she had looked, then when he raised the veil from her face how her smile had made his heart swell with pure joy and love. Their marriage vows were spoken from the heart and had an additional pledge which was the renewal of the oath they had taken three years previously when they had gone on a hiking weekend and had walked for miles on a moorland path when they stopped and gazed around in wonder at the panoramic view laid out before them. She had nestled into him, her head on his chest, hearing the thud of his heartbeat and as she turned and raised her eyes to meet his gaze they were both overcome, not only at the beauty before them but also by the intensity of their feelings for each other. They had sworn an oath to be together forever.

He flicked back to the year 1987 and soon found the photo – Tina sitting on a rock gazing out across the moors, the sun shining from a cloudless sky and a small, secret smile on her lips. He felt his heart expand the same way as it had on that day, when he felt so much love in his heart it felt boundless and eternal.

Two weeks later they had gone into a jeweller's shop and she chose a modest engagement ring, then the following year they put down a deposit on their first house together, a small two bedroomed semi-detached house with a tiny garden, but ideal for first-time buyers. They lived carefully, making sure that they could save a decent amount from their salaries to give her the wedding she dreamed of. Ben had worked for the same firm since leaving college and Tina had by then secured a place in a television studio in the marketing team of a popular TV shopping channel.

They had honeymooned on a small Greek island that wasn't overpopulated by tourists and it was almost like their own private island. For two weeks they sunbathed and swam, explored the surrounding islands by boat, went out on midnight starlight cruises and gazed into each other's eyes over candlelit suppers on the balcony of their hotel. Yes, they were so happy, so much in love and Ben felt his eyes moisten as he looked at each photograph, being able to recapture the sounds and smells and the joy of life he'd experienced at the time.

That's why he loved photography so much, it had the power to bring everything into present life – the past didn't fade when there was tangible evidence of events through the power of photographs, nor did it deceive like the mind did. Life was captured as it was then and held forever. He had often said to Tina if the house was burning down the first thing he would save – after Tina of course – would be the cabinet holding his boxes of photographs! He often spent hours just looking through them, as he was doing now, and already he felt a renewed purpose and energy to change the direction of his marriage to try to bring Tina away from the path of self-destruction she seemed to be on.

When he looked at his watch he was astounded to see that three hours had passed. The sun had moved away from the front of the summerhouse and was now shining through the side window but partially screened by the large sycamore tree, so it was still hot. He left the door open and went back down the garden into the kitchen. Tina still hadn't returned from her shopping trip, which he guessed would take at least another hour if she was meeting her friend for coffee, so he decided to make another coffee and go back into the summerhouse and spend the rest of the afternoon with his photograph collection. It had the power to relax him and ease his worried mind – it was his sanctuary, his place of refuge.

He was sitting cross-legged on the floor in the summerhouse with the boxes of photos all around him when Tina came home. He looked up to see her walk down the path with a tray with two cups of coffee and a plate of biscuits. He smiled as she entered and she flopped down on the large bean-bag chair after putting the tray on the table.

"What are you doing?" she asked.

"Nothing, just looking through old memories," he replied, a rather wistful tone in his voice.

"Oh, you and your photographs!" said Tina with a dismissive flick of the wrist. She was quiet for a few moments, then she said, "Do you fancy doing something tonight?"

"Like what?" he asked without looking up.

"I don't know………maybe ………go for a drink somewhere?" she asked tentatively.

"We could go for a walk, if you fancy it?" said Ben, "Maybe down the towpath along the canal? I'll take my camera."

"Mmm! We could call in at that pub up by the bridge," she replied.

"Well, maybe on the way back – let's have a decent walk first, it's a lovely night," said Ben, trying to accommodate both activities – he didn't want to walk just over half a mile and spend the rest of the evening sitting in a pub, but he would welcome something to drink if they'd walked far enough to create a thirst! He glanced up and saw the flicker of annoyance cross her face so he quickly changed the subject. "Did you get the shopping okay? Did you meet up with Sarah?"

"Yes," she replied standing up, "I'm going indoors, it's too hot in here. I'm going to take a shower to cool down, and maybe have a little nap. I've bought quiche and salad for the meal tonight, it's too hot to cook."

"Okay," he replied and he watched her as she walked back down the path to the kitchen, *I bet she's feeling fragile after last night's session,* he thought and felt a twinge of annoyance mixed with a tiny feeling of gloating that she was suffering, but quickly stifled such a malicious thought! That was one of the problems when one partner had a drinking habit – it affected the other person in the relationship! It was bringing out characteristics in him that he didn't like.

He knew that her asking if he wanted to do something tonight was her way of trying to get him to go with her so she could have another drink – hence her flash of annoyance when he suggested a walk first. If they didn't go out, she would open and drink a bottle of wine at home, maybe two bottles and he would either go back down to the summerhouse or go into the spare room where the computer was and play games. He wouldn't sit in the lounge with her after she'd consumed a couple of glasses of wine – that's when she started to get scornful and disparaging and they would end up saying bitter things to each other.

Tina went into the kitchen and filled a glass with water. *Oh, boy, do I feel rough!* she said inwardly as she gulped down the cool, fresh water. She smiled as she remembered some of the antics they had gotten up to last night – her, Sarah, Mandy and Louise, all work colleagues but more like sisters as she often told them. Tina was an only child and had grown up in quite a sterile home environment – neither of her parents were demonstrative or showed any feelings and although she never felt unloved she always felt that something was missing from her childhood. When she and Ben became an item in their last year at school, she felt that she had found the missing piece and as their love grew, she thought she was complete - until she started working in the studio and became part of the marketing team.

It was a pressurised job and the norm was to unwind over a drink or two at a nearby wine bar most lunchtimes or after work. At first Tina didn't join in – she would go with them all, but she would sit with a soft drink as she ate her lunch. Every time they arranged a night out they would invite Tina, but she always declined saying she always went out with her husband.

"Oh, we don't go out on the pull," said Louise, "My old man would put his foot down if he thought we were up to anything! No, we just have a sing-a-long and dance – and a good laugh – and we DO have some laughs, don't we, girls?" They all echoed her views and nodded vigorously.

They then started to tell Tina about some of their capers and she had to admit it sounded like good, innocent fun and something she had never experienced before. She had never gone out on a girls-only evening, apart from a hen party when someone got married but that was somehow different because it had a reason. It was at her own hen party when she got drunk for the first time and that was partly due to the girls from work plying her with drinks but mainly her own impulsiveness. They kept urging her to drink, telling her it was her last night of freedom and she rashly agreed as she downed another vodka and pineapple. It didn't seem to register with her that she and Ben had been living together for almost two years, so she wasn't losing any freedom at all.

The next morning she paid the price for her enjoyment and couldn't get out of bed except to be violently sick. Ben was worried and sat in the bedroom, scared to leave her alone in case she was sick while she slept, but once she stopped vomiting she slept soundly so he dared to go downstairs and make something to eat. She slept for most of the day and when she finally came down into the kitchen, she looked ruefully at him saying she would never drink again.

Then after they came back from honeymoon and she and Ben had settled into their domestic routine, she asked him one night if he minded if she went out on Friday night with the girls from work. She said they did it most weeks as a way of de-stressing and none of their husbands objected. Ben was fine about it and the first few times she came home she was quite sober as she remembered vividly how hungover she felt from her hen party, and so she only ever had two drinks all night long. It seemed to happen gradually – she had another drink because she was thirsty and had danced a lot, then she felt the sense of alcohol-induced joy, then it became several drinks before she felt 'happy' until it became a competition of who could drink the most and their drunken giggles determined the night's success.

The four of them became really good friends and shared a lot of intimate secrets as only best friends do. At the works' Christmas party where partners were invited, Ben didn't really hit it off with the other husbands and partners as he didn't drink the way they did. He said he was driving as that was his normal excuse when people tried to coax him into having 'just a small one', but he was met with hoots of derision as they called out, "It's Christmas! Leave the car and get a taxi! Enjoy yourself, man!" Tina kept making excuses for him, saying he was on medication, or he had a bug, then she simply admitted he didn't like alcohol - to which the girls laughed incredulously, but left him alone.

As Tina slowly went up the stairs and into the bathroom she was thinking about Sarah that she had met with today. Sarah had asked her to meet up at the coffee house in the retail park after she'd been to the supermarket as she needed to talk. She had confided in Tina that she thought her husband was having an affair. He was an up-market lawyer and dealt with many cases of divorce where his clients were rich and glamorous women and she thought that the current case he was working on was taking up far more time and energy than it should given that it was a straightforward non-contested divorce. Tina had listened intently as Sarah had bared her soul and wept as she told Tina she couldn't live without him. Tina had asked her what proof she had of his infidelity and Sarah had replied that she had none and she was scared to confront him, but she knew him and she knew when something was not right and also that he had suddenly started to have several overnight stays in London when he had driven to a conference of new legislation that was going on to the statute books. Previously, this had been an occasional occurrence and quite often Sarah would take a day's leave and go with him to spend the day in the city, but suddenly he had started saying he was car-sharing with three other members of the firm so it wasn't appropriate for her to go.

Tina thought about how she would feel if she were in Sarah's shoes and she had found out that Ben was having an affair, but the thought just didn't ring true! She and Ben were together forever – he would NEVER cheat on her, the same as she would never cheat on him. Even though they had different interests – she liked to go out with her friends and dance and drink and Ben had his photography and his computer games - they still loved each other intensely.

She had a cooling shower and draped in a light and flowing caftan she laid on the bed and closed her eyes. They'd had a lot to drink the night before, but she didn't usually get hungover now – she'd become accustomed to large amounts of alcohol. The first two drinks usually just relaxed her and then the fun bug took hold and they all took to the dance floor, drinking, laughing and dancing the night away. She loved the girls, they were the sisters she'd never had, very affectionate, compassionate and supportive and she felt fortunate to have them in her life. She also felt privileged that Sarah had chosen her to be the one to sound out her concerns about her husband's apparent infidelity, although she knew that the others would also be informed the next time they met up because they shared everything.

Two hours later she woke up feeling much better. The heaviness in her head had abated and her eyes didn't burn so much and the sun had moved from this side of the house so the room had started to cool down. She slowly got up and walked over to the window that she had opened wide when she first came into the room and looking down onto the garden she saw that the summerhouse door was closed so she guessed that Ben had gone back into the house. As she went down the stairs she could smell something cooking and when she entered the kitchen Ben looked up and said, "Ah, there you are. Do you feel better now?"

"Yes," she said, "Is there something in the oven?"

"I've put in a couple of jacket potatoes," he replied, "I thought they'd go nice with the quiche and salad – is that okay?"

"Yeah, that's fine," she said as she walked out of the kitchen door into the garden, then stopped and turned back. Going over to the wine rack she pulled out a bottle of wine and opened it. She took down a wineglass, then paused with her hand still on the shelf. "Do you want one?" she asked Ben.

He glanced over to her and said, "No, I'm okay – I've got some lime juice here." She grimaced as he said this and closed the cabinet door. She poured out a glass of wine and went back out into the garden. She sat down carefully on the patio swing seat and gently rocked back and forth, letting the cooler air fan her face. She enjoyed the peace and tranquillity their garden offered, the only sounds were coming from the delightful birdsongs, while in the distance she could hear muted children's voices, yelps of joy and laughter as they seemingly splashed and played in water in their own gardens. She sat with her eyes closed feeling a contentment that that seemed to be missing from her life on most days of the week. Her working life was hectic and high-pressured, with targets and deadlines to meet and challenges that Tina readily accepted. She was a very competitive person and her marketing strategy had helped to push her higher up the ladder in the last couple of years till she became Team Leader in the Sales Department. The team consisted of her, Sarah, Mandy and Louise as well as the two admin assistants, Laura and James.

Ben came out and said softly, "Do you want to eat out here?"

She opened her eyes and smiled at him. "Yes, that'll be nice. Do you want a hand?"

"No, you stay there and relax, I'll bring it all out."

A few minutes later he came out carrying a large tray. He placed the plates down on the little bistro table and pulled out the chairs. She walked over and took the cutlery and serviettes and placed them on the table while he put the tray on the patio floor. They sat in comfortable silence and ate their meal. Soon her wineglass was empty so she stood up to go and get the bottle. He looked up and realised immediately what she was going for and his heart sank. She'd already consumed one very large glass of wine and the second glass would be equally as large.

"Are we still going out for a walk tonight?" he asked as she came back to the table, "I've been looking forward to it."

He saw the hesitation cross her face, but then she brightened. "Yes, that'll be nice – it's a lovely evening."

He asked her about work and she talked reflectively about some of the deals they'd managed to secure and how the production team and the presenters were constantly at each other's throats, then after a while she asked him about how his work was going. He knew she wasn't really interested in his job, it wasn't exciting like hers appeared to be, but it was nevertheless demanding. He was a business analyst and spent all his working days dissecting difficulties and problems that firms and businesses acquire which prevent them from progressing and he would be tasked with finding the best way forward for that particular business to operate more successfully. He had a completely logical and pragmatic approach to problem-solving, which was why he took it so badly when he could see his marriage floundering and he knew what the cause was but couldn't seem to find a way to halt the decline! He was utterly bewildered that such an obvious difficulty in his private life could cause such havoc when intricate impediments in a business environment were an exciting challenge that were resolved with relatively minimal effort from him.

Once they had finished eating he carried the plates back into the kitchen and Tina sat back on the patio swing. When he came back out after loading up the dishwasher and tidying the kitchen, he noticed her wineglass was empty and as he bent down to pick it up, she said, "No, leave it – I'm going to have another."

"I thought we were going out for a walk?" he said, fingers of dread creeping into his stomach.

"We are! I'll just have one more teeny little drink before we go!" she said with a smile, but he knew by the flush on her cheeks and the slight slur in her voice that she was half inebriated already. She tottered into the kitchen and Ben sat down heavily on the garden seat opposite the swing, desperately trying to figure out how he could coax her to leave the wine and go for a walk. He knew if he became annoyed or irritated, or raised his voice, or showed displeasure in any way at her drinking habit, she would become hostile and bitter towards him and this would cause her to drink more then she would accuse him of driving her to it!

He got up and went down the garden to the summerhouse. He hadn't locked the door from his earlier visit, so he went inside leaving the door open wide. He put on some music and began to sort through the CDs in the cabinet trying to take his mind off what would be the most likely outcome from this evening and not focus on the acute feeling of disappointment that was curdling in the pit of his stomach. Half an hour later there was no sign of Tina so he went back into the house hoping she had gone upstairs to get changed for them to go for their walk but knowing deep inside that this wouldn't be the case.

As he walked towards the lounge he could hear a music channel on the television blaring out dance music and Tina sprawled on the sofa, the wineglass held up high above her head as if in tribute and the empty wine bottle lying on it's side on the floor as she sang at the top of her voice accompanying the song that was on the screen, her eyes fixed on the ceiling. Ben walked to the front of the sofa and stood directly in front of her, his arms akimbo.

"I thought we were going for a walk!" he said loudly because of the volume coming from the television.

"Don't shout at me!" said Tina, her brows furrowing.

Ben walked over to the television and turned it off. "I was only shouting because the music was so loud," he said with supressed annoyance. "Are we not going for a walk, then?"

"I'm tired," said Tina plaintively, "You can go, if you want, I'll just stay here." She slid her legs off the sofa and tried to stand up but lurched sideways and Ben had to grab her to prevent her from crashing into the glass coffee table. The wine bottle skittered across the floor and Ben bent over and picked it up before that too smashed into something. He sat down heavily on the armchair as Tina tottered out of the room her wineglass clutched to her chest, her caftan billowing out behind her and a few moments later she was back, another wine bottle in one hand and her wineglass in the other.

Ben looked up as she came back into the room. "Why won't you have a drink with me, Ben? You never do!" she said accusingly.

"I don't drink, Tina, you know that. And you know how I feel about it, look what it's doing to you!" He stood up, his feelings of disappointment and anger making his voice harsh. "You're becoming an alcoholic!"

She laughed loudly, waving the wine bottle towards him. "Because of this? I'm an alcoholic, because I like to drink wine?" She laughed again. "I've never missed a day of work, have I? If I was an alcoholic I wouldn't be able to work, would I? You're just being pathetic!" Her voice had risen and the bitterness had crept in. "You're so boring – you don't do anything I like to do!"

"Tina! You don't DO anything except drink wine till you're drunk, then fall asleep! How is that exciting?" Ben had raised his voice to match hers, then with a hand to his forehead he marched past her out of the door. He knew there was no point in pursuing this line – they'd been here so many times before and he didn't want it to end up how it usually did with her becoming aggressive and saying hurtful things.

He felt a pressure inside his chest and he made his way down to the summerhouse praying that she wouldn't follow him to prolong the argument and once inside he closed the door and sat down heavily in the beanbag chair. He held his head in his hands and allowed the feelings to wash over him, hot, scalding ears bursting from his eyes as he sobbed into his hands.

He couldn't go on like this! She definitely had a drinking problem – maybe not an alcoholic, but she had a problem! She wouldn't acknowledge it, so there wasn't much chance of her doing anything about it, he knew that much – a person had to own a problem before they could seek a solution. She had changed so much over the past four years that he hardly recognised the woman he was living with! He rocked slowly back and forth, self-pity consuming him and allowing himself to wallow in it. When his tears eased, he wiped his eyes and face on the bottom of his tee shirt and took a deep breath in, exhaling slowly till he felt himself in control of his emotions.

He took out his photograph boxes. He picked up the box of his previous life before Tina – his early childhood, his parents, summers with his cousins at Auntie Vera's caravan in Skegness, photos of the Boy's Brigade – a group photo of them all in uniform just before he went to his first camp. He had a wistful smile as he looked at all the faces, trying to remember all the names, wondering what they'd done with their lives. Most of them were just memories, only two of them were in his current life – George Blakely who was an accountant and was married to a librarian - he'd met them at a Charity function he had gone to a few years ago, and Adrian Forsythe who was a pharmacist in the large chemist shop in town and had never married but stayed at home to look after his elderly mother.

Soon he was feeling more composed and as the sun had dropped behind the trees, the garden was in shade. He decided to mow the lawn and do a spot of tidying in the garden – he needed to do something physical to expend the pent-up feelings still inside. He spent the next couple of hours doing that then when the garden looked clean and tidy and the smell of newly cut grass filled the air, he sat on the patio swing and looked around with satisfaction. He turned his attention then to what state Tina would be in, but he already knew the answer to that – she would be passed out on the sofa in the lounge!

With a heavy heart he went inside and after washing his hands at the kitchen sink, he went into the lounge. Sure enough, there she was, head lolled to one side, wineglass lying on her chest, the second empty wine bottle on its side on the floor. With a deep sigh, he took the wineglass from her and picked up the bottle and placed them on the coffee table. He started to shake her awake, calling her name.

"Tina! Tina! Come on, wake up! Let's get you up to bed!"

She snorted and flailed her arms at him. "Gerraway!" she mumbled, "Lea' me alone!"

"Okay!" he said, "You can lie here! See if I care!" He whirled on his heel and went out to the kitchen. Why didn't he just leave her there? Chances are she'd just sleep it off! *But what if she's sick?* said the tormenting voice inside his head. *She won't be!* his rational brain argued back, *she'll just sleep till morning!*

He went back into the lounge. Looking again at her unconscious, motionless figure he decided he would leave her there. He couldn't face the hassle of getting her up the stairs, so he walked around the room, making sure there was nothing left switched on – no television or music centre nor anything she could hurt herself with if she woke through the night and leaving a small lamp on in the corner so she would be able to see if she did wake, he went up to bed. *I feel more like a carer than a husband,* he thought to himself, *I would never have pictured our marriage ending up like this!*

His thoughts drifted to his work schedule on Monday. He had a new client to see at eleven o'clock, but he had a final report to sign off first. He knew Michelle, his private secretary, would have it ready for him, even though it wasn't due for another week. She'd joined the firm three years ago and was such an asset to him at work - he often thought how lucky he was to have her working with him. They'd become quite close in the last few months – she seemed to understand without asking when his spirits were low and knew it was because of something that had happened in his private life even though he never talked about his home life at work.

She was a quiet girl who had the most amazing smile. It was the norm for all the PA's to receive a decent Christmas gift and Ben wanted to get Michelle something different because she'd worked so hard for him, so last Christmas he'd bought her two tickets for a spa day and evening at a country hotel, and on opening the envelope she had smiled at him so dazzlingly that he was rendered speechless for a moment.

"I…err…..thought you could take someone….. a friend…….or boyfriend ……….or someone……", he stuttered.

"Oh, thank you, Ben, I'll take my sister!" she said clutching the tickets to her chest. Ben gathered from this that she had no boyfriend and a few weeks later when they had a late night at work one Friday and he offered to take her for dinner when she stayed with him to help collate the figures for a presentation he had the following Monday, she told him bits about her private life.

She'd told him she lived with her sister Lydia who was eight years younger than her and who suffered terrible bouts of anxiety ever since their parents had died in a horrific car crash five years ago on the motorway when they were travelling back from a weekend break in London. Lydia was fifteen at the time and had been unable to take her GCSE exams because of the trauma and so she was unqualified for any kind of work and this compounded her low self-esteem and bouts of anxiety. She had recently been introduced to mindfulness and meditation by her counsellor and was making great improvements, so much so that she was also preparing her to do some voluntary work in an animal rescue centre who were experienced in helping people who suffered problems with their mental health.

Ben was intrigued by her story and often asked about Lydia's well-being. He knew that Lydia went to her meditation classes on a Tuesday and a Friday, so for the past couple of months he had often asked Michelle to have dinner with him, knowing she would be alone till Lydia came home at ten o'clock. He always said it was because they'd worked so hard and they deserved to unwind a bit, but he began to realise that Michelle eased his own loneliness as Tina went out with her work colleagues every Friday without fail.

Michelle had confessed to him one night that she actively dismissed any advances from would-be suitors because of her commitment to the welfare of her sister and told Ben that she wouldn't expect any man to take on this extra responsibility. Ben assured her that there would be someone out there that would gladly do this – it was much the same as a man taking on a wife who had children to a former partner, but Michelle smiled fondly at him and he knew by her eyes that she didn't believe it.

A few weeks later, as they were preparing dinner, Tina asked him if he was going out the following night – Friday.

"Yes, I'm going for a bite to eat then a few drinks with a colleague from work. Why?" he asked her. He'd asked Michelle to go for a meal with him after work, but obviously didn't tell Tina this.

"It's just that we can't meet up tomorrow – Sarah's gone to her sister's for a week, Louise is on holiday and Mandy's husband is in hospital so she'll be visiting him."

Ben didn't reply but carried on with setting the table.

"Can't I come to the pub with you?" she asked him.

"Not really – it's just the guys from work, and we don't stay late, I'm usually home by ten o'clock."

"Why can't I come with you?" she asked, "We haven't been out together for ages – I could meet you and you could introduce me to your colleagues."

He wasn't acting when he flushed red and started to mumble excuses because he hadn't really planned for this possibility, but when she got suspicious and started to badger him, saying he never took her out for a drink anymore, so why was he so keen on going with his workmates to the pub, he held up his hands in surrender.

"Okay! Okay! I won't go then, I'll come straight home and stay in with you!"

"That's not what I want!" she shouted, "I want to come with you to the pub!"

He took a deep, steadying breath and looked her fully in the eye. "No, Tina! I don't want them to see you getting drunk!"

"You're ashamed of me!" she cried as if not believing what she was hearing.

"Yes, I am!" he said very quietly. Her mouth was agape and she stood with the pan in her hands, poised to transfer the vegetables onto the serving plate. "I can't live like this anymore, Tina," he continued, "I see other people having a good time without having to get drunk and I don't want to live like this anymore."

"So what are you saying?" she demanded.

"Just that! I don't want to live like this anymore!" He dropped his gaze to the floor. He was telling the truth – there was nothing coercive or manipulating about how the conversation had turned – he didn't want to live like this anymore.

"You don't understand how stressful my life is!" Her voice had started to crack and she blinked furiously as she placed the pan down on the kitchen worktop.

"It's your drinking, Tina. That's what the main problem is. If you could control your drinking, we wouldn't be where we are." He was watching her carefully, feeling that this time she was actually hearing what he was saying.

"So, you want me to give up alcohol altogether? Am I not allowed even one glass of wine?" she said petulantly

"But that's the problem – you can never stick to one glass of wine!" said Ben.

"But if I do, then that's okay?" she asked.

"Tina, I don't want to lay down rules for you – I never have! You make your own decisions, I want you to decide to stop after one glass. I don't want to monitor what you're doing, that's not how our marriage works." Ben was busy trying to salvage the meal, while Tina pondered over what he was saying.

"Okay! I'll show you how controlled I am! I'll have one glass of wine with my evening meal and just go to bed!"

"I don't mind staying in with you tomorrow," he offered, but she shook her head.

"No, you go out, no point in both of us missing out with our buddies!"

The following evening as he and Michelle sat in the restaurant his thoughts drifted to Tina at home and he wondered if she had managed to stick to having one glass of wine. Michelle noticed the distant look in his eye and asked him if everything was alright. He smiled wistfully at her, thinking how different he felt when he was with Michelle and felt a rush of gratitude that towards her for her calming presence in his life.

"I'm sorry," he said, "I just let my thoughts wander for a minute – it's nothing for you to be concerned about." They chatted some more about Lydia's volunteer work which was giving her valuable work experience, and how her mental health had improved tremendously since she began working at the pet rescue centre. Ben loved to hear about Michelle's home life and often thought how different his life would be if he had a wife like Michelle – that's how he had envisaged his and Tina's life together – still enjoying simple things and exploring new interests together like they once did, not wasting weekends on alcohol binges and fraying Ben's nerves with her self-indulgent and antagonistic behaviour.

They dawdled over coffee. Ben didn't want the night to end and felt a growing fondness for Michelle. He even pictured the kind of life they would have together – always taking Lydia's needs into consideration, too, but then Michelle looked at her watch.

"I'm sorry, Ben, but I'll have to go – Lydia will be home soon and I don't want her to come home to an empty house. She doesn't know where I am."

"That's okay," said Ben pulling himself up sharply, "I need to be getting back myself. I'll get the bill."

They walked to the carpark behind the restaurant and Ben held the door open for her to get in the car. As she passed him he had the urge to kiss her but restrained himself because he knew it was from feelings of gratitude more than anything else. On the way home they chatted about the deadlines that were coming up the following week and how far on Michelle was with the final reports. When he reached her house – a modest two bedroomed semi in the corner of a quiet cul-de-sac – she got out of the car and bent over to thank him.

"Goodnight, Ben, and thank you for a lovely meal," she said softly.

"You're very welcome," he replied, "I'll see you on Monday – have a good weekend and, Michelle...........take care."

She gave a little wave as he turned the car and drove slowly away. He always felt at peace when he'd spent a social evening with Michelle and he had a growing awareness that she was becoming perhaps more than a work colleague. He still had a contented smile on his face when he drew up outside his own front door next to Tina's car but then his thoughts turned to inside the house and he wondered if Tina had managed to just have one glass of wine.

The light was on in the lounge and he could hear music playing. Tina was on the sofa fast asleep and he could smell the musty, fruity smell from the wine. The empty wine bottle lay on the floor, the empty wineglass lying next to them.

"She couldn't do it!" he said brokenly, his face contorted with disappointment and grief. He walked round the sofa so he was facing her and gruffly shouted to wake her up, but she was dead to the world. With tears smarting in his eyes he picked up the wine bottle and glass and took them into the kitchen. As he went to place the bottle in the recycling box his eyes rested on the two bottles left in the wine rack. She'd gone through two bottles while he was out, and it was just after ten o'clock.

He went back in the lounge, took the throw from the back of the sofa and placed it roughly across her, making sure she was lying on her side, then went up the stairs with his heart almost breaking in two with the realisation that he was witnessing the death of his marriage.

The next morning he came downstairs to find her in the kitchen cooking breakfast. Her hair was dishevelled and she was wearing last night's clothes, but she looked alert and happy. "Sorry about last night – I fell asleep towards the end of the film I'd been watching," she said as she placed a plate of bacon, eggs, tomatoes and toast in front of him.

"No, Tina, you fell asleep because you drank two bottles of wine!" he said angrily. "You couldn't stop at one glass, could you?"

"I didn't….." she began, but he cut her short.

"Don't lie – that makes it worse! I noticed how many bottles there were last night and there are two less now. So you drank two bottles of wine! Again!"

He sat down at the table and angrily pulled the plate towards himself and began to eat, trying to force each mouthful past the lump in his throat. Tina didn't speak, but with her eyes lowered she began to butter the toast on her plate.

Ben put his knife and fork down and breathing slowly and carefully, he recited the words he had rehearsed since last night.

"Tina, I told you on Thursday – I cannot live like this any longer! Before you jump to conclusions, I haven't been unfaithful, but there is someone I like. Someone who likes to do the things I do and who doesn't feel the need to get drunk all the time!"

Tina jumped up. "I'm not listening to this!" she cried and ran out of the kitchen.

"No! Come back. We need to talk!" he insisted, but she had run upstairs and locked herself in the bathroom. Within minutes he could hear the shower running. He went into the bedroom and sat on the bed, waiting for her to come in. Fifteen minutes later she walked in wrapped in a large bath sheet with a towel round her hair. She was startled when she saw him sitting on the bed and he spoke as soon as she entered the room.

"Tina, we have to talk, I want to tell you………."

"No!" she cried, "I'm not listening! I don't want to hear what you're saying!" and she turned and ran back into the bathroom, turning on the small shower-radio that hung on the back of the door.

Ben went downstairs. He felt deceitful – he was letting Tina think there was someone he was interested in. It had occurred to him last night in bed that when he thought about how he felt when he was with Michelle, he realised that perhaps she was someone that he could be interested in! He had told Tina he hadn't been unfaithful, it was important that she understood that nothing had actually happened with anyone else – he was trying to use shock tactics! More than anything he wanted her to stop getting drunk but if it cost him their marriage, he would make that sacrifice, but he knew for certain that he couldn't live like this any longer.

Later that day Tina was sitting in the coffee shop near to the supermarket and nursing a cappuccino while she tried to get her head around what Ben had started to tell her – he had found someone he was interested in! He said he hadn't been unfaithful – yet! She brooded on who it could be and where they must have met!   She couldn't believe that Ben would ever look at another woman, they'd been together for almost all of their lives! How could he even think about another woman? She felt the tears prick her eyelids and she blinked furiously. She got up and gathered her bag and went out of the coffee shop. She thought the best thing to do was to push it out of her mind and focus on the groceries, but that turned out to be more difficult than she thought – she didn't care about food, she had no appetite so trying to find food to make interesting meals was too much of a challenge.

She gave up in the supermarket and made her way home. She was worried when she saw his car wasn't there – where could he be? She put the groceries into the fridge and cupboard and went back to the car to bring in the box carrier of wine bottles. As she stacked the bottles in the wine rack, she made another resolution to curb her drinking – she would make a determined effort this time. It didn't occur to her to not buy wine – she hated to see the wine rack empty, so she resolved to make one bottle last the entire week. That would show Ben she could do it! Last night was a mistake – she'd forgotten that she'd made that promise, but she would do better from now on. And she wouldn't come home steaming drunk when she went out with the girls from work. She couldn't let Ben leave her! He was her life – she didn't know life without Ben! They'd been together since she was fifteen – that was seventeen years ago!

She heard his car pull up outside and relief flooded through her. As he came into the kitchen she smelt the fresh clean smell of him and she noticed the glow on his face and the brightness of his eyes.

"Where have you been?" she asked him carefully.

"To the gym – a workout then a swim afterwards!" he said quietly.

She was silent for a moment, then suddenly her voice rose. "Is that where you met her? Is she one of the lycra-cladded bimbos that struts around the gym pretending to exercise but scared to break a manicured nail if they actually DO any exercise?"

"Don't be silly, Tina, I go to the gym to exercise – we ALL do! If you bothered yourself to come and DO some exercising, you'd see that the people who attend really care about their health! And if they've got good bodies, it's because they've looked after them!"

He was trying desperately to hang on to the feel-good feeling he always achieved when he'd pushed himself hard at the gym, but he could feel it slowly evaporating as if being melted by the heat from Tina's wrath. He walked through the kitchen and went down to the summerhouse and unlocked the door. He put some country music on the CD player and took out the photograph box from his last photography course.

While he was at the gym he was thinking about enrolling on a digital photography course as digital cameras were becoming more affordable now and he had decided to ring up the college on Monday to ask for a prospectus to be sent to him. He was browsing through some of the photographs he had taken, mainly wild-life and was inwardly congratulating himself on achieving some stunning shots, particularly of the birds, when he saw Tina stalking towards him.

"I thought you'd be here – with your beloved photographs!" she snapped.

"What do you want, Tina," he asked tiredly.

"I didn't want to know – but now I do! Who is she? Who are you having an affair with?" Her face was red and she was breathing heavily, and Ben could smell alcohol on her breath. He dropped his head onto his chest. He wished he'd not said anything.

"I haven't been unfaithful – I'm not having an affair!" he said slowly and carefully. "I said it because……..there are lots of people who have fun without getting drunk! There are lots of people who can have just one glass of wine with or without a meal and be content with that."

"So why did you say there was someone you were interested in?" she snapped, "You wouldn't just make it up – there must be some truth in it!"

"I was trying to shock you – to let you see that………it could be a possibility! There are people all around me who are interesting people, who don't have to drink alcohol till they pass out!" He was feeling really uncomfortable now – he'd led her to believe he was interested in someone – he'd actually envisaged Michelle while he was saying it, but he hadn't ever talked about personal feelings with Michelle – she might not even like him!

"Well, I think you're trying to control me! I think you're using emotional blackmail to force me to do what you want!" she snapped.

"Tina! That's ridiculous!" He was astounded that she could come up with something as ludicrous as this and he could feel the gulf between them widening. Where was she getting these ideas from?

"So…… if I said I wanted to go out tonight, you wouldn't try and stop me?" she asked him defiantly.

"I've never stopped you going out, Tina. All I've asked is for you not to drink yourself into a stupor!" He suddenly felt too exhausted to care anymore. "Do you know what – do what you want! I'm sick and tired of trying to keep you from harming yourself – and then to be accused of trying to control you! Well! Do what you want! I've had enough! I can't take anymore!"

He pushed past her and stormed up the garden path and through the kitchen door. He heard her scream of rage, then a loud clatter and as he entered the kitchen, he looked back to see she had swept all his photos off the little table and they lay scattered on the floor then she had picked up the box and threw it at the wall.

He felt a rage build up inside him. He was extremely slow to rise to anger normally and could count on one hand the number of times in his life he had been enraged, but he could feel a burning resentment inside him and he knew he had to get away from her. He grabbed his car keys and slammed out of the front door. Perhaps a couple of nights in a hotel would give them both the breathing space they needed.

He drove through town and parked at a motel just off the feeder road to the motorway. There was a pub across the road and he walked across to it, feeling the cool air from the overhead ceiling fans as he pushed the door open. A few people glanced up as he walked in, but nobody paid any attention to him. He ordered a beer at the bar and took it to a corner seat where he sat nursing it while he tried to take stock of what he was going to do next. He rarely drank alcohol, but he needed to think and he didn't want to look out of place so he sat with a glass of beer in front of him. He needed to calm himself before he did anything else.

He tried to analyse how he was feeling, how the last few years had gradually eroded the love that he had towards his wife. When he took Michelle out for meals after work, there was honestly no ulterior motives – it began as gratitude for extra work she had done for him. She was a work colleague and that's how he saw her and it was by chance that she reminded him of Tina as she used to be many years before. It was when he went home and saw Tina in a drunken stupor that he began to make comparisons and resent the person Tina had become and imagine coming home to someone like Michelle. He couldn't visualise Tina going back to the sweet, gentle girl she used to be – she seemed to have undergone a personality transformation and become a selfish, brash, alcohol-dependant aggressor that he didn't even like!

After a while when he was feeling more composed and he had thought through the dilemma he was facing, he had reached the conclusion that staying away for a couple of days was the best way to progress then maybe he'd be in a position to make a decision about their future. Tina was extremely volatile these days and he wouldn't be able to have a calm discussion with her, so this was the best way forward. He gulped a mouthful of the beer then left the half-full glass on the table.

He walked back across to the motel and entered the door. He knew this was a decent and reasonably priced motel as many of his clients had used this when they came into town for a meeting. He gave the receptionist a story about finding his home flooded and needing somewhere to stay for a couple of nights till it was sorted. The receptionist, feigning interest, took his details, asked for his signature and his card details and gave him the key. He said he would go and collect a few personal items and would be back within a couple of hours.

As he got back into his car, Ben steeled his mind against any regrets at his own impulsiveness and as he started the car he rationalised what he was intending to do. It was only to give them some breathing space – he wasn't leaving her, he wasn't giving up on his marriage just yet! This was a last-ditch attempt to SAVE his marriage.

When Ben had stormed away leaving Tina in the summerhouse, she had swept her arm across the table, sending all the photos flying in all directions in her rage. Then she slumped down on the floor and with tears pouring out of her eyes she wept bitterly, feeling the rage still burn inside of her. How could he say he'd met someone he liked more than her? He was going to leave her and go with someone else! She couldn't let that happen. She leaned across and pulled out the long box from the cabinet and placed it on the table in front of her. This was the story of their life together. She sniffed and sobbed as her fingers trailed over each section, all lovingly created by Ben. He loved his photograph collection.

She started to pull out random photos. For each photograph she picked up she could recall the detail of that occasion – the smells, the sounds, the sights – all of their holiday photographs showed a couple in love, a man gazing tenderly at his wife, she in turn looking up at him adoringly. Their wedding photos – her tears came faster as she looked at them, her beautiful dress, she looked like a princess from a fairy-tale and he, her prince. All brides look beautiful, but she had FELT beautiful on that day! That magical day almost seven years ago!

They had shared so many good times, they had laughed together so much, even the last holiday they'd taken last summer ……………although they weren't together so much on that one, most of the photographs were of picturesque little villages or panoramic views when Ben had gone walking by himself when she was lying in bed nursing a hangover from too many cocktails the night before - apart from those that they took at the poolside, but on a lot of them Tina was asleep! They had each taken turns – one posing and one taking the snap, but she could remember how happy they had been……..they had *always* been happy. How could he say he didn't love her – here was proof that he loved her. She collected the photographs together and put them back into the box, leaving the box on the small table in the summer house, tears pouring down her face

When he arrived back home, he cautiously went in through the front door. He could hear music playing loudly from the lounge and as he pushed the door open he could see her swaying in the centre of the room, a wineglass in her hand and a flush on her cheeks. He shook his head slowly and walked over to the music centre and turned the volume down. She whirled around.

"What do you think you're doing?" she demanded.

"Tina, listen to me! I've booked into a motel for a couple of nights – to give us breathing space. We need to be apart for a while till we take stock of what's happening to us!" He was talking slowly and carefully, so that she would understand what he was saying.

"You've WHAT? You're going to HER, aren't you?" she shrieked, "You're leaving me for HER!"

"There is no HER, I've told you! I didn't mean it, I was trying to shock you!" He was pleading with her, willing her to calm down, trying desperately to undo what he'd done by uttering that foolish comment.

"Well, you're not going! I won't let you!" she yelled and ran round the sofa to slam the door closed and stand with her back to it, the wineglass still in one hand and the other arm stretched out across the door.

"Tina! Let me pass, don't do this! I'm only at the Premier Inn, just for a couple of days till we both can think more clearly." He tried to take her arm to move her but she shrugged him off and gulped down the remainder of the wine in the glass then threw the glass across the room. It hit the wall behind the television and shattered to the floor. He had impulsively ducked as he saw her arm go back and when he heard the sound of glass breaking he quickly glanced across, but then turned to her and took both arms and pulled her away from the door.

"I'm going to pack some things and go – DO NOT try to stop me!" He had raised his voice in order to be heard above the roars and screams that were coming from Tina's mouth. Her eyes were blazing and her face was contorted in anger.

He roughly yanked her to one side and pulled the door open then bounded up the stairs to the bedroom. He grabbed a small case from the spare bedroom then marched into their bedroom and pulled the wardrobe doors open. He hastily selected a couple of clean shirts for work, some razors, toiletries and underwear and zipped his suit into a garment carrier.

Tina ran from the lounge into the kitchen, her mind in a whirl. What could she do? She had to stop him! She paced the floor, trying to make a plan, but her thoughts wouldn't connect. She ran up the stairs, shouting, "You're not going! You're not going! I won't let you!"

Ben heard her running up the stairs and put his foot behind the door to prevent her from coming in. "Tina! Stop! It's just for a couple of days! It's the only way! It's the only way we can sort this out!"

She screamed again and ran back down the stairs. She put her hand on the top of her head, pulling at her hair. She had to stop him! What could she do? She ran back into the kitchen, pulling out drawers and opening cupboards randomly, not knowing what she was looking for but frantic to find something to stop what was happening.

She ran back outside down to the summerhouse and wrenched the door open. She grabbed the box of photos and lugged them back up the path staggering under the weight, wanting to show him their happiness. Wanting him to see how happy they were – it was there on hundreds of photos – proof that they were happy together. The box was too heavy and the weight of it pulled her down tipping out the photos all over the ground and causing her to graze her knees on the garden path and take the skin off her knuckles. She was crying and sobbing, the pain in her heart far greater than the pain in her hands and knees as the blood trickled down her legs. She picked up the empty box and threw it madly into the open door of the summerhouse, screeching in her anger and frustration

She ran back into the house and up the stairs. "I'll show you!" she screamed at the closed bedroom door, "I'll show you!" then ran back down again into the kitchen. She clutched her head and looked around her, her eyes darting from one side of the kitchen to the other, pulling out draws again at random.

When Tina saw the match box lying in the bottom of the kitchen drawer, she knew with an absolute certainty that this was the answer – the only answer. She picked it up and with a trembling heart she shook the box, relief flooding through her veins when she heard the sound of rattling inside. She frantically opened the box and with her breath quivering in her throat she looked through her tears at the contents - matches, their small red tips promising a solution to end her heartache.

With sudden clarity she knew that this was the only way – he couldn't just walk away from her and give his love to someone else as if she didn't matter anymore. She couldn't be constantly reminded about the love they had once had by seeing him – seeing his face, the face she had always loved, the face that had told her he was leaving her! She placed the matches on the kitchen bench and scrabbled in the bottom of the cupboard under the sink. There they were – firelighters!

She ran into the hall and grabbed the bannister at the bottom of the stairs ready to run up and confront him again, but then she heard him shouting from the garden, "What have you done?" and as she darted back through the kitchen she was just in time to see him go into the summerhouse. She grabbed the matches and firelighters and raced up to the summerhouse door and slammed it shut, turning the key in the lock and as he turned, his arms instinctively came up to ward off blows as he heard the noise. She waved the matches and firelighters at him through the glass door.

"This will teach you a lesson," she shrieked.

His face blanched. "Tina! What are you doing?" he yelled, raw fear in his voice, "Open this door! Tina!"

She laughed manically and shook the matchbox again, then took out a match and struck it. "You think you can just start your life again, do you? You think you can just leave me and walk away? Well, you're NOT! You are NOT!" she bellowed and shook out the box of firelighters on to the ground, then snatched one up, waved it at him, then set the match to it. The flames took hold immediately, racing round the small white brick causing her to drop it on the path. She could hear him screaming in terror through the summerhouse door, "NO! Tina! What are you doing? Stop! Open the door! Let me out!!"

She quickly piled one firelighter on top of another until there was a fierce blaze. Ben was hammering on the door, making the glass shudder, but it was double-glazed so it withstood his hammering. She could hear his bellows, shouting at her to open the door but she ignored everything in her frenzied state.

She ran to the photos and began scrabbling on the floor to pick them up and throw handfuls of them on top of the flames, hearing Ben shriek, "NO! STOP! Tina! Not the photos! Tina! Not that! There's no going back from that, Tina!" But she laughed manically and continued, the fire becoming larger as the photographs flared, curled then perished, the record of their life together disappearing in acrid black smoke. She turned to face him, her face red and swollen, her eyes like narrow slits and a look of triumph on her face.

Ben was pressed up close to the door, both hands on the glass panels where he had been pounding his fists and tears were pouring down his cheeks, shock mingled with loathing written all over his face. He shook his head slowly in disbelief and horror at what she had done, then as the last of the charred photographs curled up and disappeared, she sank to the floor in exhaustion, weeping pitifully.

She turned towards him, shaking her head slowly and deliberately.

"It was the only way," she whispered, "You were destroying our future – so I destroyed our past! I've wiped it out – as if you didn't exist! It was the only way!"

*****

Long Lost Love

Abbi arrived ten minutes early for the Yoga class as instructed by the text message she'd received from Carrie earlier that afternoon, saying she had news for her. Carrie was already there and as Abbi walked into the changing room, she came running towards her and grabbed her arms, pinning them to Abbi's side and pushing her into a small storage room at the side of the studio.

"I've found him!" Carrie said in an excited tone, "Your long-lost love! I've found him!"

"Whaaat? How?" gasped Abbi, "Are you sure it's him?"

"I'm sure!" laughed Carrie gleefully, "I told you I could do it! Well, I've done it!"

Abbi sat down heavily on the bench and gaped at her friend. There was a group of four of them and they'd been coming to Yoga for the past several years and every month or so they met up for meals or nights out together, often reminiscing about their youth or past loves in their lives. Carrie had been happily married for eleven years now and hadn't found her 'Mr Right' till she was thirty-nine, Mel was fifty-six, divorced and happy to be single and Noreen had been married since she was twenty-two and had four children who all had young teen-age children of their own. Abbi had been widowed for almost seven years since her second husband had died tragically in a car accident and she had two grown-up daughters.

A couple of months ago they'd been out for afternoon tea and the chat had turned again to favourite times of their younger days and Abbi had talked again about her first real love when she was sixteen, a young man called Adrian Lumley. She'd told them about his gentle nature and his courteous behaviour and how at that age she'd wanted more of a 'bad boy' image because that was what all her friends at that time were into, and Adrian's gallantry made them laugh and make fun of her. She'd said that now she regretted how she'd behaved towards him and would give anything to be able to meet up with him again, but she had heard a long time ago that he had emigrated.

Carrie had immediately said, "Do you want me to find him for you?" and Abbi had laughed and said, "You really think you can – after all this time? This was over forty years ago!"

"Abbi, Abbi, have you not heard of social media? You can find anybody these days no matter how much time has passed!" Carrie was a techno-genius whereas Abbi still preferred the old-fashioned methods of communication and didn't indulge in social media at all.

Now, today, Carrie was telling her that she'd traced him!

"Oooh! You mean it's actually him? How do you know – how can you be sure?" Abbi's face had grown pink and her eyes were large as she looked at Carrie.

"His name is Adrian Lumley, he was born and raised in North Shields, he's now sixty-five, marital status divorced, he worked as a plumber in the shipyards on the Tyne then when he was twenty five he went to New Zealand. He returned to England when he was fifty-eight and is currently living in Durham!" Carrie had a smug, self-satisfied look on her face as recited these facts, then she rummaged in her massive, oversized bag till she brought out a sheet of paper and waved it in Abbi's face. "This is a printout of the private messages that I sent him - to which he promptly replied!"

Abbi gasped and snatched it off her. The first message was the one that Carrie had sent introducing herself, outlining her mission and asking if he knew Abbigail (nee) Henry please respond and if he was agreeable she would forward the message to Abbi.

Just at that moment, the Yoga teacher walked through the door calling for everyone to come in ready to start the class. Abbi's heart was racing and she pushed the paper into her bag as they walked into the changing room and stowed it in the locker. The grin on Carrie's face almost lit up the room as she walked into the studio and Mel and Noreen both looked at her and said, "What've you been up to? You're like the cat that's swallowed the cream!"

"Tell you later!" she grinned mischievously as she shook her yoga mat out and winked at Abbi. They all focused for the next hour on their yoga practice, all except Abbi, whose mind was anywhere except in this room.

She'd met Adrian at a local dance-hall when she was with her friend Susie and at the end of the night he'd walked them both to the bus-stop. He was extremely tall and fair haired and chatted easily to them both, then just as the bus appeared at the bottom of the road, he'd grabbed her hand and said, "Meet me tomorrow, at Newcastle bus-station, half-past seven? Please?" She'd looked at her friend but Susie was busy fiddling with the strap of her sandal that had snapped as they came out of the dance-hall.

"Okay," she replied, "I will." She smiled nervously at him and turned to get on the bus. He stood waving to them as the bus pulled away, and as she turned away from the window

Susie said, "Are you going on a date with him – I heard you said 'okay'?"

"Yes. Tomorrow. I'm meeting him at Newcastle bus station at half-past seven. He's nice, isn't he?"

"He's alright, I suppose," sniffed Susie, "Not my type!" and turned her face to the window of the bus.

Abbi smiled. She always said something like that when one of their group got a date and she didn't, but 'her type' didn't seem to be very much different to theirs - and they all swooned and raved over the same pop idols.

Abbi had met him the next day at the bus-station in Newcastle – she'd arrived twenty minutes early as she didn't want to look for him, she'd rather let him approach her. He was also ten minutes early so by twenty past seven they were deciding where to go. He was so tall that she had to lean back to look up at him and he had a loud, deep guffaw that took her by surprise each time he laughed, which he did a lot – he always found something to be amused at.

That night they went to the cinema and he bought her a box of chocolates! They came out after watching some film that she couldn't follow but which contained some extremely funny scenes and Adrian's laugh could be heard throughout the cinema, causing a few to turn their heads and snigger.

Abbi had been more interested in the chocolates – she'd never had a box of chocolates bought for her before - apart from Christmas or birthdays! Once outside he'd asked her where she would like to eat and she'd said, "I don't know……..you choose!" trying to sound as though it was something she did regularly.

He'd led her to an Italian restaurant asking if that would be alright, and she'd nodded not trusting herself to speak. She'd never been in an Italian restaurant – she could count on one hand the number of restaurants she'd been in and none of them as posh as that one. She'd gazed around in wonder and allowed herself to be led to a table in the corner adorned with a flickering candle and attended by an obsequious waiter. She'd felt so grown up, so mature.

Every date after that had followed a similar pattern – he had treated her like she was something precious. He'd always worn a suit and tie, he'd opened doors for her, he stood up when she left the table, he always made sure she was on the inside when walking along the pavement – she'd felt like a queen when she was with him. Her mother adored him, her sisters fawned over him, her friends ridiculed him.

"Where you going tonight with Mr Good Guy?" Shelley had asked as they came out of work one Friday, "Another

night of holding hands and gazing at the stars? Doesn't he
bore you to death?"

"Who's this?" Susie had asked as she strode in front of
them stretching up as high as she could with her arms flapping
by her side giving a little skip as she bent forward and gesture
outwards with her hand saying, "After you, ladies," then giving
a raucous belly laugh causing the people in front to look back.

They'd all laughed and giggled to Abbi's
embarrassment and she'd shouted, "That's not fair! He's a
really nice lad with really good manners!"

"He's not a lad!" scoffed Shelley, "He's too soft – he's
more like a lass!" They'd all laughed again and Abbi's cheeks
burned. She hated it when they did that, and the more she
had defended him, the worse the teasing got, so she always
ended up being silent.

She went out with him for over two years – they only
ever met on a weekend as he had his bed-ridden mother to
care for through the week and on a weekend his sister, Pam,
who was a nurse working night shifts, took over allowing him
time to spend with Abbi. On the occasions that Pam wanted a
night off Abbi would go to their house and sit with him as he
attended his mother's needs, then they would watch television
together. It was a gentle and virtuous relationship – he never
had the roaming hands that most young men suffered from, he

would kiss her passionately, but then pull away and tell her he wanted to keep her pure! It was so different from what her friends were saying that their young men got up to.

Their ridiculing had finally got to her and she told him one night as they sat in a coffee house that she wanted to finish with him. He looked at her in horror. "But why? he asked, "What have I done?" There were tears in his eyes as he begged her to give him another chance, whatever he was doing that she didn't like, he would change it, but please don't end it. How could she tell him that it was because he was too nice – his only problems were perhaps that his legs were too long and she kept falling over them when he was sitting relaxing, and his laugh was too loud and he laughed too much and people looked at them, and her friends all thought he was too soft and they teased her mercilessly about him! He treated her like she was precious china and what she really wanted was a bit of rough-handling like her friends talked about – not hurting them but showing how manly they were. How could she tell him that?

She couldn't answer him so she got up and ran, out of the coffee house and out of his life. This was long before the mobile phone era, so he'd sent her letters every day begging her to reconsider, asking what he'd done wrong. After a few weeks the unanswered letters stopped coming and a couple of years later she'd met and married someone else.

Looking back now, she could see how her first marriage had been a complete disaster as she ended up with the exact opposite of Adrian – the type of man that she had thought she wanted but four years later she'd divorced him on the grounds of unreasonable behaviour. She'd heard through the grapevine that Adrian had emigrated to New Zealand after his mum had died, and she told herself she'd done him a favour by letting him go, thus giving him the freedom to enjoy his life, but many times when she was feeling lonely she would think back and wonder if she'd done the right thing in finishing with him.

Dragging herself back to the present she realised the Yoga session had finished and she hadn't been aware of any of it happening. As she and Carrie came out of the studio, they were joined by Mel and Noreen and they all stood around the drinks machine while Carrie filled them in on her detective work and Abbi read and re-read the paper that Carrie had given to her about Adrian.

"Are you going to ring him?" asked Mel, her eyes wide in excitement.

"I don't know………Oh, I'm so nervous!" whimpered Abbi.

"Yes! She IS going to ring him!" insisted Carrie, "I didn't do all that for nothing – you at least have to ring him!"

"Can't I just send a text message?" Abbi bleated.

"If you must – just get in touch with him – or else!" said Carrie in mock sternness.

"But I'm sixty-two years old! He'll be sixty-five now! We're both too old for stuff like this!"

"Stuff like what?" cried Carrie, "All I'm asking you to do is to reacquaint yourself with a former boyfriend – I'm not asking you to run off any marry him! Let's just see what happens – just ring him!"

They parted company, saying that they expected to get feedback from Abbi by the next Yoga session, and Abbi made her way to the car-park. Her heart was still beating madly when she arrived home and let herself into her house. She threw her bag on the chair and sat down heavily on the sofa taking her phone out of her pocket. She stared at it for a long while, then impulsively grabbing the sheet of paper with Adrian's details on she sent him a text message, saying that she was too shy to phone him, but this was her number if he wanted to contact her she would be free the following evening – Tuesday - if it was convenient for him. She then pressed 'send' with her heart still in her mouth!

He responded within three minutes, saying he was elated to hear from her and if it was suitable he would call her at seven-thirty the following evening. Her reply simply said,

'That's fine, thank you.'

On Thursday when they all met again at the Yoga class, she told them that she'd had a long phone conversation with him. They were all excited and bombarded her with questions that she answered as nonchalantly as she could, not disclosing the sleep deprived night she had spent after the text message she'd sent and the heart-skipping day she'd spent at work the following day. Every time she thought of the imminent phone call her stomach lurched and her heart missed a beat.

She couldn't eat her meal that night and picked at the plate before her as she watched the clock tick round to half past seven. When the phone rang her stomach flipped so hard she thought she was going to faint and when she answered the phone she was sure he would be able to hear her heart pounding in her ears. She hadn't easily recognised his voice but told herself that she'd never actually heard him on the telephone before and his voice would have changed over the years anyway. In her ultra-anxious state, she couldn't formulate a coherent sentence but he soon made her feel at ease and before long they were chatting like the old friends they were.

They both had grown-up children – he had two sons, she had two daughters. One of his sons was living in New Zealand with his mother after Adrian and his wife were divorced, the other was teaching in Thailand. Abbi told him about her first short but disastrous marriage and her second husband who had tragically died in an accident nearly seven years ago leaving her with two teenage girls and how she had lived alone since then as both her daughters were married – one living in Leicester, the other one in Southern France.

He told her he'd started a plumbing business when he came back to England – he'd had a very successful business in New Zealand, which he sold before he left and as he transferred the family home entirely to his wife, she didn't make any claim on his business so he had adequate capital to set up in business back in England.

Abbi told him she worked as a case manager in a Social Services Family Centre and gave him an outline of the various things that would happen in the day-to-day running of such an establishment.

When it got to ten o'clock she told him that she needed to go as she got up early for work. He apologised profusely for keeping her talking for so long, but she said she had enjoyed their chat – then he asked if he could ring her again on Saturday night, to which she'd immediately agreed.

Noreen was giddy with excitement whereas Mel was simply curious about how she felt after all this time and Carrie was boldly confident that they would re-ignite the passion of their youth, but Abbi stayed calm and rational, telling them that it was early days after a long separation and they were still getting re-acquainted. She promised to give them the next instalment on Monday at their class.

On Saturday evening she set the phone down on the small table near to the sofa, then she poured herself a glass of wine and set it down by the phone so she could sip while she chatted, then thought she might get thirsty so she poured out a glass of orange juice, then set out a plate of nibbles. She stepped back looking at the array set out near the phone and gave a self-conscious giggle thinking all this preparation was simply for a phone call! When the phone finally rang, she felt her heart jump painfully and made herself take three long steadying breaths before she answered it.

Adrian asked how she was and what kind of week she'd had, then after she'd told him she enquired about his week,

"I've been in a bit of a dream state this week to be honest," he replied, "I kept pinching myself to see that I wasn't dreaming about you getting in touch! For so many years I prayed for it to happen, imagined what I would say to try to win you back, and so when it did happen and we got back in touch…………. I could barely believe it!"

"Really?" she asked, rather taken aback by the intensity of his words, "But you emigrated, surely you left it all behind when you left the country?"

"That was the purpose," he said, "But I never forgot you no matter how hard I tried!"

Abbi was dumbfounded. She hadn't imagined in her wildest dreams that Adrian had carried feelings for her for all these years. She knew he was devastated when she finished with him, but she wasn't even eighteen then, he was her first serious boyfriend and she was so young, so naïve, consequently she expected him to have put her out of his mind. Now he was telling her she'd always been in his thoughts.

"Oh, Adrian, I'm so sorry. I didn't realise how much I'd hurt you. I was very young and ……….but I shouldn't have been so heartless." Abbi felt guilt pressing down on her and she berated herself for the cruel way she'd dismissed his feelings when she'd ended their relationship.

"It's okay, don't feel bad! At least you were honest with me – more than I was when I married Sylvie! I should never have married her, but it was the only way I could get you out of my mind! Only it didn't work!"

There was a deep silence as Abbi struggled to find words. But then he spoke again.

"But it all came good in the end, didn't it? I tried to find you for so many years when the internet and social media came out but drew blanks everywhere."

"No, I've never taken to social media," said Abbi quietly.

"But your friend found me, so you must have asked her to, or at least talked about me," he said and she heard his voice grow hopeful again.

"Well, yes, we'd been talking about first boyfriends and regrets and such, and she told me she was confident she could find you, so I told her to try……….to be truthful, I didn't expect her to be successful after all this time!" Abbi felt her cheeks grow pink and was glad that they were talking on the phone and not face to face.

"She was certainly successful!" His booming laugh startled her for a moment and she smiled at the rush of nostalgia, thinking she'd recognise that laugh anywhere only now she was a mature woman she wasn't embarrassed by it!

"I would really love to take you out," he continued, "I don't want to rush things, but it's not as if we were strangers that just met – we've got history! What do you think?"

Abbi was quiet for a moment. She certainly didn't want to rush into anything – she had been very happily married to Steve for twenty-nine years and would have still been with him if fate hadn't snatched him away so cruelly, but she'd been on her own now for seven years and had to admit that she sometimes felt very lonely.

"I think…….that would be very nice," she heard herself say.

"Fantastic!" he said and she could hear the pleasure in his voice. "I'll get the train up to Newcastle – can you get the train and we'll meet at Central station?"

"Yes, that's fine, there's a Metro line not far from here that goes straight into Central. We could meet under the clock like we used to – it's still there!" Abbi felt little bubbles of excitement inside her as she was talking. It didn't feel strange making these arrangements with Adrian – she had always refused to go on dates when her well-meaning friends tried to set her up as she couldn't bear to think about getting to know another man as a prospective boyfriend or partner, but this felt natural and comfortable.

"So much has changed in Newcastle, I barely recognised the place," said Adrian, "I was up there a few weeks ago visiting Ben Fulton – do you remember him? He lived a few doors away from my mam's house and I sometimes went fishing with him while his mam sat in with my mam."

"Only vaguely," Abbi said, "I remember your grandparents – that time I spilled my tea on her best white tablecloth, and she was so gracious about it, but she must have been as devastated as I was – it was her best cloth!"

For the next three hours they chatted about old times, recalling past people and events, laughing comfortably together as each memory triggered another one. As they were talking Abbi had been sipping her glass of wine and felt totally relaxed and at ease with him. Eventually, Adrian said he'd better let her go as it was eleven o'clock and he didn't want to monopolise her time.

"It's a bit late for that!" she laughed, "But it's not like I was going to do something else when I'd finished on the phone with you, I'm only fit for cocoa and bed at this time of night!"

"Me too," he said eagerly, "I do enjoy a cup of cocoa on a cold night!"

Abbi laughed out loud, "Oooh! Don't we live dangerously!"

When she saw the girls at the next Yoga class her eyes were shining and her smile lit up the room as she recounted the conversation she'd had with Adrian.

"Oh, my word!" said Carrie, "Just imagine – he's loved you all these years, even when he got married to someone else! Think we need to start looking at hats, girls!" They all giggled like teenagers, especially Abbi – she'd felt the years slip away as she was talking to Adrian and she'd spent Sunday experiencing the same rushes of excitement that she'd had when she was a teenager!

"Honestly – I couldn't concentrate in work today and had to keep checking what I was doing because my mind kept drifting!" said Abbi as she laughed self-consciously, "I'm like a love-struck adolescent!"

"Ah! I'm so happy for you – you deserve to be happy again," said Mel. "It'll be nice to meet up face-to-face then you can see if the magic is still there."

"Well, I don't know about magic," said Abbi, "We never………….got physical, if you know what I mean!"

"Doesn't matter," said Mel, "You need to meet up to see if there's a physical attraction, because if not………….you might be on a road to nowhere!"

"Listen to the Angel of Death!" said Carrie, "Of course there's going to be a physical attraction! She went out with him for over two years………….and that's when they were both fuelled by teenage hormones! It was only because he wanted to keep her pure till they were married that he refrained!"

"Well, pardon me for caring!" Mel retorted, "I was just saying……."

"It's just SOOOO romantic!" sighed Noreen, "It takes me back to when Paul and I were first going out……."

The Yoga teacher appeared at that moment and they joined the rest of the class as they filed into the studio, uncurling their exercise mats and preparing themselves for the next hour of controlled breathing and yoga moves.

Adrian sent her several text messages during the following week, friendly and prudent, telling her about interesting customers he'd had, asking if she'd had a good day, saying he was looking forward to meeting up the following Saturday, enquiring if she had any preferred places she would like to eat at, favourite foods, and so on.

When Saturday arrived Abbi spent the afternoon pampering herself and choosing then changing her mind about what she would wear. She thought back to the time when she was going out with Adrian and how he always said how pretty she looked regardless of what she was wearing. Her hair was long in those days and a rich shade of chestnut, helped by the colour rinse that gave it hints of red – now it was cropped short and dyed dark blonde to disguise the grey that covered her entire head. She'd been slim in those day, too, but now despite the fact that she walked regularly and went to Yoga classes twice a week she was carrying far more weight than she did then. She finally settled on a pair of slimline trousers and a long-line pale blue tunic-top that she knew flattered her.

They'd arranged to meet at the railway station at Newcastle – he would come on the train from Durham and they could go for a meal in Newcastle then he would take the train back to Durham where he had left his car in the station car-park. It was an easy journey for Abbi too, although she decided to get a taxi from her house to the Metro station, she could get a Metro train which took her right into the main railway station at Newcastle.

She arrived early as she had done all those years ago and hovered under the huge station clock as they had arranged. She walked up and down a few times taking deep breaths to quell the rapid fluttering of her heart and the shaking of her hands then as the time approached half-past seven she saw him striding towards her. He had the widest grin she'd ever seen on anyone and he waved madly to her, his joy unmistakable. He hadn't changed too much – he was obviously older and his hair thinner and he wore spectacles now, but he was still the same tall, thin, gangly man she had left with a broken heart over forty years ago.

"Abbi! Abbi!" he called out as he neared and she smiled at him in acknowledgement. He grabbed her hands and held them, gazing into her face as if drinking in the detail.

"Oh, my word! You haven't changed a bit!" he cried in wonder, "You're still as beautiful as you were back then!"

"Thank you," she said, "You're very kind, but the fact is – we're both forty-three years older!"

"That means nothing!" he said with a flick of his wrist, then taking one of her hands and drawing it through his arm, he led her out of the bustle of the busy railway station.

"Where would you like to eat?" he asked, then looking around he said, "I hardly recognise this place now – look at it! Things have certainly changed around her, haven't they?"

"I don't mind – you choose," said Abbi, feeling the years slip away and she was for a moment the sixteen-year-old again. Adrian laughed, and there it was – the same raucous belly-laugh that had made her cringe all those years ago! But on a middle-aged man it didn't sound so discomfiting and when no-one turned to look at him she was relieved to find she wasn't embarrassed by it!

They soon found a cosy-looking Italian restaurant and he held the door open for her to enter then confidently requested a table for two as they were greeted by the pretentious waiter just inside the door and they were led with a flourish to a corner table at the back of the room. The waiter flicked the napkins across their knees and ostentatiously produced the wine menu.

"Any wine preference?" asked Adrian as he smiled softly at her. Abbi shook her head.

"We'll have a bottle of Sauvignon Blanc, please," he told the waiter who bowed his head in acquiescence as he tucked the wine-list under his arm and walked away. He was immediately replaced by another waiter who grandly opened the menu in front of each of them with a murmur of "Sir," and "Madame."

Abbi looked back at Adrian and realised he'd not taken his eyes off her since they had sat down. She felt herself flush and smiled nervously at him.

"I'm sorry!" he gushed, "I can't stop looking at you! Honestly, you've barely changed at all!"

Abbi decided to not respond – what could she say that wouldn't sound like she was fishing for more compliments? She was grateful that the waiter had returned and after asking Adrian to taste the wine, he poured it into Abbi's glass and before he'd finished pouring Adrian's wine she had gratefully taken a sip to steady her nerves. Adrian picked up his glass and held it up in a toast.

"Here's to us" he said, "The past.......... and the present!"

"To us," she echoed.

Abi concentrated on the menu, remembering their first date and how nervous she had been and how out-of-place she had felt being in a posh restaurant, then compared it to how confident she felt in the same situation now. During her marriage to Steve they ate out fairly regularly especially once the girls had left home, plus they often had friends round for dinner so Abbi was comfortable in knowing her way around any menu.

When Adrian looked across at her and asked what she would like, she said, "I think I'll have mozzarella en carrozza, followed by risotto al funghi with chicken." She smiled at him confidently and closed her menu, and moments later the waiter was back with his electronic hand-held ordering machine, hovering at the table.

Adrian ordered Abbi's food, then added that he would have calamari followed by ribeye steak with green peppercorn sauce. After discussing his choice of vegetables, the waiter smiled and bowed slightly as he took back their menus and walked away.

Adrian leaned across the table. "So tell me all that you've done in the years we've missed!"

"Oh, gosh, where do I start?" said Abbi, "Well, I met Robbie soon after you and I………… finished and we got married after a whirlwind courtship, but it didn't last and we were divorced within four years. Six months later I met Steve and we got married when I was twenty-six – another quick courtship. But in this case we lived happily together for twenty-nine years, had two daughters who are grown up and living their own lives – Megan, now thirty-four, married to a college professor and living in Leicester and Stephanie, thirty-one, who runs a design studio with her long-time boyfriend and lives in Martigues, near Marseilles in the South of France."

Abbi couldn't help the glow of pride when she talked about her daughters – she was exceptionally proud of them. Megan had married Edward and moved to Leicester the year before Steve died and Steph was working in a design studio in Edinburgh, but both girls had been enormous pillars of strength for Abbi during the first few months. She told Adrian how both girls had stood together, their arms wrapped around each other for support as they delivered a very touching eulogy at their father's funeral, telling the church full of mourners how their father had taught them both strength and humility and that although they were deeply saddened by his death, they didn't feel they'd lost him as they both carried him deep within their hearts, and always would.

Although it had been seven years since he'd gone, Abbi felt her eyes grow moist and her voice thickened as she recounted this moving anecdote, and Adrian leaned across the table and took her hand in his and squeezed it gently. Abbi pulled herself together and took a sip of her wine.

"Now your turn," she said, "Tell me all about you."

Adrian leaned back in his chair. "Well…….. after spending a year trying to win you back and failing miserably, I devoted my time to looking after mam. Her MS got worse, her depression got worse and it was tough on me and Pam – more so her as she got very little sleep when mam was in one of her black moods so I had to rush home from work to let Pam get some shut-eye before starting her shift at ten o'clock! It sounds bad when I say this but it was a relief to all of us – herself included, when mam died – she'd had no life for over fifteen years once she got MS. She hadn't been too bad when dad was alive, but once he died………..she started with depression and soon became bed-ridden."

Adrian paused to let the waiter serve their starters and they turned their attention to the food for the next few minutes. "I couldn't accept it, you know – when you finished with me," he continued after a while. "I kept writing to you, but you never answered! I came to your house a few times and just hovered outside hoping to catch a glimpse of you, but I never did. A couple of times I gathered up my courage and knocked on the door but there was no-one in!"

"I didn't know that," said Abbi, feeling slightly uncomfortable at the thought of Adrian's attempt at stalking her, but then brushed the thought away as he didn't actually succeed in seeing her. "Why did you choose New Zealand when you decided to emigrate?" she asked hoping to move the conversation on from his unrequited love.

"When mam died ……..and by then I had gathered that you didn't want me……" he gave a little grimace, "…….and at the same time I saw an advert for plumbers wanted by a firm in New Zealand set up by a British bloke. I applied, telling myself if I heard from him I would take it as a sign that I was meant to go – and I did, so I went…….. and the rest, as they say, is history!" He gave a deep resounding laugh at this point causing a few heads to turn.

"I did really well for several years," he continued, "Threw myself into working long, hard hours every day – most weekends, too. Then I met Sylvie – the first woman I'd even been remotely interested in since you – and a couple of years later we married. I was very fond of her, but I didn't love her as I'd loved you…………"

Abbi pushed her plate away and dabbed her mouth with her napkin. "Oh, Adrian," she said softly.

"It's true, Abbi. I loved you so much – I always will. I've loved you for over forty-five years and I will love you until the day I die!" He was looking at her with such intensity that Abbi felt as though she was melting under the fervour of his gaze. She felt a rush of feeling, a warmth flooding through her veins and she reached across and fumbled for his hand. He clutched at her hand with both of his, with such love in his eyes that she felt the room grow distant and only the two of them remained, locked in each other's gaze as the years slipped away and they were young lovers once more with their future stretching out before them.

Just then the waiter returned to remove their plates and dust away any crumbs he imagined he saw and they broke apart, crashing back to reality, then moments later their second course was served so the mood was shattered.

After each of them had commented on the quality of their meal and making small talk about the décor in the restaurant, Adrian resumed his declaration of love to Abbi.

"This is fate, don't you think?" he said smiling widely at her, "That we should meet up again after all these years. I mean, you hear about it, people getting back together after being childhood sweethearts, but I never imagined in my wildest dreams I would be so lucky………..I tried so hard to find you, I dreamed about finding you!"

"When did you and Sylvie get divorced?" asked Abbi, changing the course of the conversation once more. "You said your youngest son stayed in New Zealand with her?"

"Ten years ago," he replied. "Matt was eighteen when we divorced - we were married for over twenty-two years, but then she met someone who loved her the way she deserved to be loved. I didn't contest it. So, when I said I was returning to England, Matt stayed with his mother, but Will had just qualified as a teacher and was looking to travel to Thailand and has since settled out there. We keep in touch by phone and Will came to visit me five years ago, Matt came three years ago, so they know I'm settled here. And I've got a successful business………… and I've met you again!" His face radiated happiness and Abbi felt humbled by the power she had unknowingly held.

When the meal was finished and the wine bottle was empty and they had dawdled over coffee, Abbi glanced at her watch. "What time is your train back to Durham?" she asked him, "The last one for me is at ten-twenty – I'd better start making tracks!"

"It's ten-forty for mine," he said standing up, "I'll get the bill." He beckoned to the waiter who came instantly to his side then was back moments later with the bill in a leather-bound wallet on a silver salver. Adrian laid his card on top of the wallet without looking at the bill, then turned to help Abbi put on her coat, pulling out her chair and holding her arm as she moved from the table and again Abbi was reminded of the overprotecting way he had treated her when she was seventeen. But now it felt nice. He turned back to the waiter and keyed his card number into the machine than quickly took his card from the waiter with the receipt. He returned it to his wallet and drew out a note and placed it on the silver salver as a generous tip for the waiter who smiled and bowed his head slightly as they both turned to leave.

Outside he drew her arm through his and kept his hand covering hers as they walked through the streets back to the railway station. "How will you get home from the station when this train gets there?" he asked as they walked to the overhead train timetable to find the number of the platform her train was standing at.

"I'll get a taxi," she replied, "It's only a short walk, but I don't like to walk in the dark."

"No, don't," said immediately, "And please ring or text me when you're home so I know you're safe. "

"I will," she smiled.

When they reached her platform, she turned to him to thank him for the evening, but he pulled her close into the most enveloping but gentle hug she had ever experienced. She melted into him, feeling her heart beating loudly in her ears. He pulled slowly back and then kissed her forehead and said, "Go! I'll ring you tomorrow. Please take care and let me know you're home safe."

He turned her to the doorway of the train and as he gave a gentle nudge she stepped into the train, her head in a whirl. She'd pondered since getting ready for the evening to come to meet him whether he would want to kiss her at the end of the night and whether she would respond……… but he made it all so easy for her the way he did what he did. She smiled lovingly at him as the doors slid closed and the train slowly started to pull away. She waved at him and then turned to find a seat, hoping to find one of the single seats at the end of the carriage, which she did.

When she described the evening to the girls at the next Yoga class, they were all giddy with excitement.

"Oooh! I smell a wedding!" giggled Carrie.

"Ah, Abbi, I'm so happy for you," cooed Noreen.

The expression on Mel's face was unreadable – she had a wistful, sad smile but at the same time she was expressing her joy along with the other girls and Abbi couldn't tell if she was as happy being divorced and single as she constantly professed she was.

When the Yoga class had finished, they arranged a night out together for the following Friday and Carrie jokingly said that Abbi might want to check with Adrian first.

"You're kidding!" said Abbi vehemently. "I was on my own for seven years – I'm used to arranging my own social calendar! I'm not changing that for any man!"

"We'll see!" said Carrie naughtily.

But even though she only saw Adrian on a Saturday night she was blissfully unaware of her 'social calendar' subtly changing. Apart from her Yoga class on Mondays and Thursdays and the occasional night out on a Friday with the girls from the Yoga class, her life was revolving around Adrian. She didn't see much of the group of friends from work that she used to meet up with on a Saturday night. They had been going out once a month on a Saturday night for the past couple of years – some of the younger ones had families at home and their arrangement was that the husbands went out on a Friday night and the wives went out on a Saturday night and it had worked well.

Three months had quickly gone by and one Saturday night Adrian had taken her to an expensive dinner-dance hosted by one of his contractor friends who was raising money for a charitable cause and he had insisted on taking her home by taxi. He had driven to Abbi's house and left his car there and they went to the dance by taxi. He was initially intending to drive back home after he had taken Abbi back home in a taxi, but he had consumed too much alcohol and he normally didn't drink very much, so he said he would stay in the taxi to go home then come back by train the next day to pick his car up. He added that they could possibly spend the day together – maybe go to Hexham for the day?

Abbi was appalled at how much the taxi would cost him and even though she knew he was fairly well off financially, she shuddered at the likely cost.

"Well, if we're going to Hexham tomorrow, it seems silly you going all the way to Durham and back here again tomorrow. Why don't you just stay? You can have the spare bedroom."

"Thank you, darling, that's so kind. But I haven't got any casual clothes – I would have to go out dressed in a suit and tie………. and I haven't got a toothbrush or any clean underwear!" he said holding her close as the taxi glided quietly towards them. He gently helped her into the car and seemed to fold his long legs into the car as he eased in next to her. He gave the driver her address and settled back in the seat with his arm around her shoulders, kissing the top of her head.

Abbi was full of mixed feelings. She was slightly irritated by Adrian's attention to detail – a toothbrush and clean underwear……….surely he could improvise for one day! Then there was also a tinge of resentment that he didn't leap at the chance to spend the night in her house – she hadn't invited him into her bed, she wasn't sure if she was ready for such a commitment yet, but she would have liked him to at least………..try to persuade her? For a moment she was catapulted back into the past when Adrian's virtuousness had irritated her but she quickly smothered those feelings reminding herself that he was a genuine gentleman!

When they got to her house, he asked the driver to wait as he wanted to continue the journey to Durham and the driver nodded in agreement, happy at the prospect of a lucrative fare. Adrian walked with her to her door and gently turned her to face him.

"I've had a wonderful night, Abbi," he said stroking her face as he gazed at her.

"Me too," she said, "Thank you so much for taking me, I enjoyed meeting some of your friends and colleagues."

"I was the proudest man in there tonight," he said, "You were the most attractive woman in the room!"

"I don't think so," laughed Abbi self-consciously, "But thank you for saying that."

He leaned forward and gently kissed her on the lips, then kissed her forehead as he usually did. He dropped his arms and said, "Off you go. Close the door and lock it, and I'll see you tomorrow – about eleven o'clock? We could have lunch in Hexham and go for a walk along the river."

Abbi smiled and nodded then went into her house, locking the door as he instructed before going into the kitchen and putting the kettle on to boil to make a cup of tea before going up to bed. She felt slightly guilty about feeling annoyed earlier that evening over Adrian's constant vigilance when they were at the dinner-dance. He had been talking to someone at one point so she went to the wash-room to freshen up her make-up and on her return he had looked anxiously at her and said "Where have you been?"

She looked taken aback and told him where she'd been and he said, "I was worried – next time tell me where you're going." She felt a flush of irritation and wanted to snap at him that she'd led an independent life for the past seven years, but even when she was with Steve, she didn't find it necessary to tell him of her every movement! Where did he think she'd been for, goodness sake! But she simply tightened her lips and looked away. He quickly put his arm around her and kissed the top of her head as if he guessed she was peeved.

At the Yoga class the following Monday she told the girls about the dinner-dance and the lovely evening she'd had, omitting the tinge of oppression she'd felt when she'd gone to the Ladies Room without telling him and his subsequent viewpoint. She quickly told them about their pub lunch in Hexham and the river walk where they'd chatted comfortably all day and where she'd forgotten all the misgivings she'd had the night before.

"So, did he stay over on Saturday night?" asked Carrie with a knowing smirk on her face.

"No, he didn't – he came back on Sunday," said Abbi, grateful that the instructor had called them in as she didn't want to say that he'd taken a taxi all the way to Durham when his car was outside rather than spend the night with her – in the spare room, of course.

"Well, it'll happen soon," said Carrie.

The following week when they were on the phone, Adrian suggested that they go out on Sunday again adding that he wouldn't be drinking so he could drive back home on the Saturday evening.

"You know you're more than welcome to stay in the spare room, Adrian," Abbi told him. "It seems such a waste travelling back to Durham just to return the following morning."

"I suppose it makes sense," he said after a long pause.

"Don't worry – I won't take advantage of you!" said Abbi half joking, but with a hint of sarcasm.

"The thing is……..I suppose I'm being overly cautious," said Adrian haltingly, "But it took me many, many years to get over you last time and so I suppose I'm ……….scared to take things to the next level……………if we did and it didn't work out this time ………I think it'll kill me!" he ended in a rush.

"Oh…………. I see," said Abbi, then she was silent for a few moments. She felt a crushing weight of responsibly descend upon her shoulders – how could she guarantee their future together? Then she pulled herself together. "Adrian, I only offered my spare bedroom – I didn't offer my body!"

"Oh, sweetheart! I'm sorry! Forgive me – I didn't mean to be forward, I know you were just being kind…………" She could hear the panic in his voice and was immediately mollified, but then he continued, "But……….please promise me, if it happens…….if we do………..take it to the next level, you have to be sure, very sure that it's what you want."

"I will," she told him, "But we can continue to enjoy each other's company in the meantime, can't we?"

"We certainly can!" he said, "Now, how do you fancy a trip to the cinema on Saturday evening – how about we go for an early meal then a late showing?" They continued discussing what was showing at the cinema and by the time the conversation was at an end it was as if Adrian's earlier disclosure hadn't happened.

The weeks rolled on by and soon it was Christmas. Abbi had invited Adrian to spend Christmas Eve, Christmas Day and Boxing Day at her house where she would cook Christmas lunch for them. On the previous weekend Adrian had taken her to a large garden centre where they had chosen a Christmas tree and they had spent the Saturday evening decorating it together, then the following day he had helped her to trim up the windows with flashing fairy lights and place a large plastic snowman and Santa figure in the garden. They had laughed and joked together as they did it, reminiscing about the Christmases they'd had as children and then talking about the Christmases they'd spent with their own children.

On Christmas morning Adrian insisted on cooking breakfast for them both and afterwards they lingered over coffee enjoying the Christmas songs playing softly on the radio. They then sat in front of the Christmas tree and opened the small pile of presents they'd bought each other. Adrian had bought her a bottle of her favourite perfume, a luxurious scarf and gloves, boxes of sweets and chocolates, a silver chain necklace and an expensive handbag that she'd admired one day when they were window shopping. Abbi had bought him his favourite after-shave, leather driving gloves, a sweater and a box of chocolate brazil nuts. Abbi poured them both a sherry to sip while she was cooking after she'd ushered Adrian into the lounge to relax in front of the TV with his drink.

She called him into the kitchen to carry the turkey to the table then handed him the knife so he could carve the roast. He beamed at her, saying how he had always wanted to be the man who carved the turkey but Sylvie had insisted on doing that job herself telling him there was a particular way to carve meat. Abbi watched him as he clumsily hacked off pieces of meat and thought to herself that Sylvie actually had the right idea! But she was prepared to humour him for this one day – and she wasn't too bothered about the roast, she always got fed up with turkey after a couple of days.

They had a very pleasant day, both of them feeling relaxed and content with life. Abbi opened up a bottle of cream liqueur while they snuggled up together on the sofa watching Christmas movies, and this on top of the bottle of wine they'd consumed with their lunch meant she was feeling very warm and slightly fuzzy-headed. Adrian looked at her, a lopsided grin on his face.

"Are you a teeny bit drunk?" he asked.

"No……..well, just a teeny tiny bit!" she giggled, the red flush on her cheeks giving her away.

"I think I might be as well," Adrian said and hiccupped, looking aghast as his hand flew to his mouth.

Abbi laughed uproariously and grabbed the bottle. "Let's have some more, it's Christmas!" she giggled and went to pour them both another drink. Adrian slid his arm around her back and pulled her to him as she leaned across to fill his glass and taking the bottle from her hand, he placed it on the coffee table then kissed her slowly, his other hand stroking her hair. Mellowed by the effects of the alcohol, Abbi responded immediately and wrapped her arms around him, holding him close to her. He was such a highly-principled person, so gallant, so chivalrous…………she felt her head spinning and knew that with Adrian she would be looked after, he would always care for her – hadn't he said he would love her till the day he died? She felt a surge of love wash over her and when Adrian tried to pull away, saying, "Abbi……you need to be sure……" she pulled him back into her arms and surrendered to the heady emotions that flooded her as she whispered, "I'm sure, Adrian, I'm sure."

When the holiday period was over and the girls met again at the Yoga class, Mel was already there when Abbi arrived.

""How was Christmas?" Abbi asked as she took off her coat and folded it in her locker.

"Aw! Fabulous!" said Mel and described her visit to her sister's house in a village just outside Stoke-on-Trent, where she had spent the Christmas period with her sister and her husband and children. It had been an active time, the children were young teenagers and were always on the go, coaxing Mel into all kinds of outdoor pursuits. "I've had to come home for a rest," laughed Mel.

"Ah, that's lovely," said Abbi, "We had a quiet time – just the two of us, though we had a nice long walk on Boxing Day."

"How are things going, then?" asked Mel just as Carrie came crashing in through the door.

"Yep! Good!" Abbi nodded her head up and down and looked away.

"Is this…….? Have you………?" Carrie looked from Mel to Abbi then back again, and Mel's eyes grew wide.

"You have, haven't you?" she grabbed Abbi's arm and Abbi's cheeks reddened and she turned her full attention to her locker.

"Oh, my word! Noreen, Noreen," called Carrie as Noreen walked in, "She's gone to the next level – she's done the deed!"

Noreen's eyes grew wide as she looked at Abbi, then they all laughed as Abbi put her hands to her reddened cheeks and bowed her head.

"Oh, honestly, what are you all like?" she huffed, "I'm not a teenager, you know, I'm a ………….. mature person." She stuffed her bag into her locker and picked up her exercise mat ready to go into the Yoga studio followed by the others, still giggling and making comments about weddings and hats.

"Oh, I'm SO happy for you!" whispered Carrie as they walked into the studio and Abbi felt the tears spring to her eyes as her heart sank to the floor.

How could she describe the anguish she was going through? How could she put into words the turmoil that was inside her head? How could she tell them about the number of sleepless nights she had gone through after Adrian had gone back to Durham when the holiday period was over? She didn't understand it herself, how could she expect her friends to understand?

On Boxing Day morning she had woken up and turned towards Adrian lying next to her to find he was awake and looking at her with a smile on his face.

"Were you watching me?" she asked sleepily.

"I was," he sighed contentedly. "Oh, Abbi, you can't believe how many times I've yearned for this – how many times I've pictured this happening............and now it's real, it's actually real!" His eyes were so full of love that Abbi felt a lump in her throat and tears pricked at her eyelids. She felt humbled by his love.

They went for a long walk after Adrian had cooked breakfast for them. They drove to the coast and walked along the seafront, Adrian's arm around her shoulders and her arm tucked around his waist. It was a bright, sunny morning, although very cold but they were both well wrapped up against the biting North wind and Abbi was surprised at how many people were also out walking.

Adrian had been talking about his business, telling Abbi how it operated, describing the staff he had and the types of work he undertook and Abbi was trying to focus on what he was telling her. She guessed that he was trying to show her that he was solvent, that his business was flourishing so that he could have a comfortable retirement in a few years. She had told him that she wasn't ready to retire for a few years yet – she would have a good work's pension when she did, but she loved the work so she wanted to keep going as long as she felt motivated to do so.

"I reckon in about five years we'll be ready to retire," said Adrian and they stopped and looked out across the sea. "I want us to travel and enjoy life when we do retire," he said looking down at her.

She smiled. "I'll be sixty-seven by then," she mused, "You'll be coming up to seventy! Oh, my word! How did we get so old?"

"Nonsense! That's just the number we'll be! Inside we're still young! We've got a lot of catching up to do for the years we missed." He pulled her to him and kissed the top of her head. "Oh, how I love you!"

He suddenly turned towards her and after glancing around, he dropped to one knee and took her hand. "Abbi, I've finally got you back and I can't risk losing you again. Will you marry me? Please say you'll marry me! I love you so much."

Abbi gasped. "Adrian! Get up! Don't……" She looked around in a panic.

"Not until you say you'll marry me!"

"Yes, okay, now get up!"

Adrian staggered slightly as he arose and as he regained his balance he laughed, his loud bellowing chuckle fortunately carried away on the wind. He pulled her to him in a fierce embrace then kissed her fervently on the lips. "Oh, Abbi, I'm so happy – I'll always look after you and protect you and care for you………I love you so much, I've loved you for most of my life and I'll never stop loving you!"

"I know," smiled Abbi, "And I love you." She had a tinge of guilt when she said that, but then rationalised by telling herself how could she not love someone like him – so caring, so gently and with enough love for both of them!

They went looking at rings the following day and Abbi chose a five stone diamond half eternity ring. She already had her engagement ring from Steve that she had slipped on to her right hand when she had taken off her wedding ring that morning. It didn't seem right to wear Steve's rings once she had accepted Adrian's proposal, and she mentally apologised to Steve as she slid it off and placed it lovingly in her jewellery box.

She had deliberately chosen an eternity ring style rather than a solitaire diamond ring – it felt more appropriate somehow, but it needed to be resized so they'd left it at the jewellers to be picked up in two weeks. She hadn't told her daughters yet – no doubt they'd be astonished at the speed that this had happened, so she had the next two weeks to tell them about Adrian's proposal – she'd found it difficult enough to tell them that she was going out with someone, only finding it slightly easier because Adrian was a boyfriend from her youth who had come back into her life rather than a man who was new in her life.

She told them about his proposal on New Year's Day when they rang her and was surprised but thankful that each of them was happy for her and they both promised that they would make every attempt to get to see them as soon as possible. They'd met Adrian when they came for a flying visit on separate occasions - Megan and her husband at the end of October when it was half-term and Steph and her partner at the beginning of December. They'd both given positive comments in their opinion of Adrian, neither of them in any doubt that he would care for their mother.

"He's a very nice man," they had both said as they went back to their own lives.

She hadn't mentioned anything to her friends at Yoga – she was going to just wave her hand in their direction next week when she was in possession of the ring. Adrian had booked a table in an expensive restaurant for the following Saturday, requesting a table that would offer them privacy as Abbi had stipulated she didn't want a fuss or people looking at them and there he would just slide the ring onto her finger across the table in a candlelit corner and they would drink champagne to toast their future together.

Adrian finally went back home on the Saturday morning at the end of the Christmas break as Abbi had told him she needed to give the house a good clean and catch up on washing and ironing before she went back to work on Monday. Adrian's business had been closed for the holidays but he also needed to spend time preparing and getting things in order ready for work to begin on Monday. He was reluctant to leave and Abbi was getting frustrated as she was already figuring out what needed to be done and she just wanted to get on with things. When he finally left, she closed the door with a sigh – and that's when the big wave of apprehension and foreboding swept over her.

Her mind was in a turmoil all that day and that evening when Adrian rang her, telling her he missed he so much and couldn't wait till the time came when they didn't have to say goodbye – when they were married – and the sense of dread became very real. They had loosely discussed the practicalities of marriage and the options they had, but bottom line was that his business premises were in Durham and he had employees to consider, whereas she worked for Social Services and could possibly get transferred, or look for another job, maybe part-time. They could both put their properties up for sale and look for another house, or he had suggested that she could sell hers and move into his. She had visited his house with him a couple of times over the holidays when he went to check everything was okay, and it was nice enough – very masculine at present, but she knew she could make it look the way she wanted. But she didn't dwell on it much – they'd only just got engaged, there was plenty of time to talk about marriage and where they would live.

But spending every moment with him over the Christmas period had given rise to some mild irritations already and she remembered in her teenage years how her friends had ridiculed him for being 'too nice'. She reluctantly admitted that it was truly the case – he was so nice, so caring, so genuine that it somehow felt unnatural and what she wanted was to see a bit of annoyance, or frustration, or just tetchiness – *anything* that would show he was human with human failings. Then she reprimanded herself for such uncharitable thoughts – that's the kind of person he was – why could she not accept him as being almost perfect? Why was she trying to take away his gentleness and replace it with bad moods or irritability when he didn't actually experience any of these feelings? He always found a positive in any situation, nothing ever seemed to get him down.

When she'd married Robbie all those years ago, he was foul-tempered so often that he'd terrified her and when he began to get physically threatening she'd left him before he could become actually abusive. Steve, in comparison, was very gentle and easy-going and they rarely argued, but after the children came on the scene and he had toddlers making demands on his time and energy, he started to show signs of irritation and was often prone to sulks. At first she tried to coax him out of his grumpiness but as the years went on she ignored his huffy behaviour and let him come out of the sulk when he was ready. It rarely lasted more than a couple of days and he was so contrite when he came back to his normal happy self that she immediately forgave his petty moods – she was very prone to hormonal changes herself so she often flew off the handle with him.

Adrian didn't show any signs of ever being annoyed with anyone – he constantly said, "Each to their own", or, "We're all different", or, "Different strokes for different folks".

By the time she'd got to work on Monday morning she was exhausted – she'd tossed and turned all night trying to clear her head. She was trying to put a finger on what was really bothering her. All she could come up with – the same as when she was a teenager – was that he was 'too nice'! That was ridiculous now – it might have been acceptable in a seventeen-year old with her first real boyfriend and very little experience of life, but as a sixty-two year old with two marriages behind her, being 'too nice' sounded ridiculous!

Carrie was so happy for her – they all were! They had a vision of her and Adrian settling down together, being happy ever after, a joyous reunion after forty-odd years of being apart, and now that they'd consummated the relationship, marriage would follow as sure as night followed day! Why was she plagued with doubts and recriminations?

She was very busy at work for the following week and could push her private life to the back of her mind, and when Adrian phoned her on an evening telling her silly stories about things that had happened she ended up giggling and laughing and always felt a rush of deep affection especially when they had to say goodnight. It was in bed when she turned the light off that the niggles of doubt crept in.

When Saturday came, Adrian arrived and they had a late breakfast together before setting off for the town to pick up the ring. When she tried it on she had to admit it looked beautiful – she had treated herself to a manicure the day before as she wanted to send a photograph to her daughters of her ring so she wanted her hands to look as nice as they could, given her age. Adrian then took her to buy an outfit for that evening and shushed her with a kiss when she said she didn't want him spending more money on her. He was beaming with happiness and kept patting his breast pocket where the ring was safely tucked away till that evening.

That evening, once they had ordered their food and the bottle of champagne was standing in the ice bucket at the end of their table, Adrian took the little velvet box out of his pocket and with his gaze fixed firmly on Abbi's face he opened the box and took out the ring. He leaned across the table and took her hand, then slowly slid the ring onto her finger.

"Oh, my darling, I've loved you since I was nineteen years old and I have spent my life wishing for a moment like this," he said huskily holding on to her fingers. "Now that it's happened I feel so emotional……….please don't ever leave me - I spent forty-three years without you and I couldn't go through that again! I think it would kill me to lose you!"

"Oh, Adrian," said Abbi tenderly, "I've never been loved so much…….."

"No-one could love you more than I do," he said vehemently, interrupting her but then gently kissed her fingers. He looked across and gave a small nod to the waiter who then slid noiselessly to their table and lifted out the champagne bottle which he draped in a small white linen towel. He expertly popped the cork and poured the sparkling liquid into their glasses and as he did he said quietly, "Many congratulations to you both," and with a small bow he backed away from the table.

Abbi's heart was full and she kept looking at the glittering ring on her hand, smiling lovingly at Adrian as they sipped the champagne. The meal when it arrived was sumptuous and they chatted easily, talking about things that had happened at work until gradually the conversation got round to their future together.

"Let's not wait too long to get married," said Adrian, "We need to decide whether we're selling our houses and getting something else, and where we want to live. Obviously, I have my business to take into consideration, so I'd like to stay in Durham……..or not too far away," said Adrian.

Abbi had a fleeting moment of panic but then quickly rationalised it as her life-long anxiety about change – any change!

"There's no rush," she said carefully, "I mean, we were talking about being ready to retire in less than five years – you'll be selling the business then, so it won't matter."

"Do you mean we should wait five years to get married?" he said in a surprised tone. "I couldn't wait that long – I've waited long enough!"

"No, I mean we don't need to live near your business as you'll not have a business in a few years – couldn't you sell it earlier – retire younger?" Abbi asked.

"I suppose," said Adrian, pouring more champagne into their glasses, "What about you? Would you retire earlier?"

"I need to work for four years for my state pension," said Abbi.

"But you'll have your work's pension, and if we both sell up and buy something else we should have some spare change out of it to give you a bit of security," said Adrian with a warm smile. "Let's do it! Let's sell up now, houses AND my business, get married, retire and live happily ever after!"

"Woah, woah, slow down," laughed Abbi, "We've only been together seven months, we don't have to rush into anything."

"I've waited too long already," Adrian said decisively, "Now that I've finally got you, I want us to be together for the rest of our days!"

Just then the waiter came to ask if they wanted coffee and Adrian said, "Yes, please, we'll have Irish coffee."

Abbi would normally not drink coffee so late at night, but as this was a special night and Adrian was being so lovingly assertive, she didn't make an issue of it. The champagne was making her feel relaxed and slightly light-headed and she could tell that Adrian was also feeling the effects of the champagne and was glad that they had taken the decision to come by taxi rather than drive as she guessed he would not be fit to drive home at the end of the evening.

The next morning Abbi woke up to the smell of frying bacon and as she slowly made her way downstairs, she could hear him singing as he moved about the kitchen. She walked in the room tying the belt of her dressing-gown, conscious that she must look the way she was feeling.

"Good morning, my love," Adrian boomed as she cautiously pulled out a chair and sat down at the table holding a hand up to her head. "Oh, dear me, are you feeling a bit fragile?" he asked, concern etched across his face.

"I'm afraid I am," she replied in a low voice, "I don't normally drink champagne, or Irish coffees late at night."

"Well, here you are," he said, plonking down a glass of water and two paracetamol tablets. "This'll fix you – I felt a bit rough same as you when I got up, but I'm fine now, so get them down you, eat your breakfast and you'll be right as rain in no time." He turned back to the worktop and continued buttering the toast, then placed a plate of bacon, eggs and tomatoes in front of her, a large mug of coffee and a plate of hot buttered toast.

The irritation Abbi had felt when she first sat down soon dissipated as she munched her way though the breakfast and she reminded herself what a kind, caring man Adrian was. Many women would give their eye teeth for someone like him, she told herself and the little voice inside her head whispered, *'Keep telling yourself that!'*

When she went to her Yoga class the following day, she was quite eager to show the girls her engagement ring. Her work colleagues had been quietly astonished at the appearance of the ring as she had always kept her private life very private, but sure enough her Yoga pals were ecstatic, hugging and squealing and wishing her many congratulations. When the class was finished and they were collecting their bags from their lockers, they arranged a night out on the Friday as Abbi had told them she and Adrian weren't having an engagement party.

"We'll have to make sure we keep in touch if you go to live in Durham," said Carrie and Mel and Noreen agreed with her. "Aw, we'll miss you!"

"We might decide to live here, not Durham," said Abbi, "Nothing is decided yet, we're discussing options – we might both retire early, who knows what we'll do? It's funny – I thought my life was laid out, I expected to work for the next four years then perhaps take a part-time post before retiring fully. Now I'm considering early retirement……………to be honest, I don't know if I'm ready to retire just yet – and I don't know if I want to give up my life as I know it!"

"What! You've got to be kidding!" said Mel and Carrie together, "What an opportunity for you," continued Carrie, "You and Adrian could go travelling, or do anything you want to do – he must be worth a bob or two!"

"I know what you mean," said Noreen quietly, "My mum stopped working when my dad retired and she became depressed – she couldn't handle not having a routine or a purpose any more. It was awful – I'm sure it hastened her death. You have to be ready to retire to be able to enjoy it."

Abbi nodded and smiled warmly at Noreen. "Yes, exactly……..thank you, Noreen."

"Well, let's discuss it on Friday when we meet," said Carrie, "You and Adrian will have had time to chat about things, so you might have more idea of what you want to do with your life. I'm still pretty thrilled for you……….. you deserve to be happy."

Abbi spent a week agonising over her future. She was having a particularly successful time at work – a lot of things she and her team had been working on since the end of last summer were beginning to come to fruition and she had been given a lot of praise at her supervision session. She was feeling very contented with life, but then would remember that she might be giving it all up soon and her stomach would lurch at the prospect. When Adrian phoned her on a night, he was so full of positivity and eagerness that she felt quite exasperated by it and wanted to snap at him, but she refrained and just tightened her lips till the feeling passed, but then he would be so loving that her resentment soon melted.

When Friday came and she entered the Bistro, she saw that the girls had already arrived and Noreen spotted her and waved as she crossed the room towards their table. Abbi shrugged her coat off and draped it over the back of her chair as she sat down and the waiter immediately asked if she wanted a drink. She ordered a soft drink as she was driving and then noticed that the girls were all waiting expectantly for her to speak.

"What?" she asked, looking round at each of them.

"How's it going?" asked Carrie, "Have you and Adrian come to any agreement about your future together?"

"Not really," said Abbi, "Do you know………… Oh, forget it! I'm not in the best of moods at the moment!" said Abbi and Carrie leaned forward and laid her hand on Abbi's arm.

"What's the matter?" she asked softly, "This is not like you. Has something happened?"

"Well, yes – I got engaged after seven months to a man I used to go out with forty three years ago who I finished with because ……I don't know……..he was too nice….. and now I'm going to give up my job and sell my house and marry him and live………I don't know where and probably have to lose all my friends because I'll be travelling to God only knows where ………and………." She stopped as the tears rushed to her eyes and spilled down her cheeks before she could do anything about it.

The girls were all taken aback and rushed to comfort her all at the same time whilst trying not to draw attention to their table, but Abbi pulled her hands away as she groped in her handbag for a tissue.

"Sorry, sorry," she mumbled, "I'm just getting fraught with everything…….."

"Is work getting you down?" asked Mel.

"No, on the contrary," sniffed Abbi as she pulled herself together, "It's going really well – there's some really good stuff going on at present and my manager is very pleased with our results. I'm getting a lot of job satisfaction just now."

"Typical!" said Noreen.

"You don't have to rush into anything," said Carrie, "Adrian loves you – he'll wait for you, he'll wait until you're ready."

"Yes, I know," said Abbi, "It's just………..oh, I don't know………do I really want to get married? I was happy the way I was!"

"No, you weren't!" contradicted Carrie, "Do you remember the conversations we had – and there were several, where you yearned to meet up with him again, how you regretted how you'd treated him, couldn't forgive yourself for the mean way you'd been with him and how lonely you said you felt on long weekends when you didn't have your job to keep you busy!"

"That's because I missed my daughters……" said Abbi, but Carrie shook her head.

"No, it wasn't the girls you missed, it was a man's company – it's been over seven years since Steve died, and you said yourself you'd been thinking more and more about Adrian as time went on. Now the Universe has handed him to you……….. you're just scared of change!"

The waiter came and took their food order and created enough of a disruption to end the conversation that was beginning to cause a sense of discomfort for Abbi. Once the order had been taken and the waiter retreated, Abbi looked around at them,

"I'm sorry, I'm behaving like a spoilt child. You're right, Carrie, I AM scared of change – I always have been! I'm sure it'll all work out……"

"Of course it will," said Noreen, "I mean, this is a fairy-tale, isn't it? When true love conquers all."

Abbi pursed her lips and took a deep breath in. "That's what I don't know……….. whether it IS true love! I know *he* loves *me*….……….in fact that's what's scaring me, it's almost………….too much!"

"What do you mean?" asked Carrie in consternation. "Does Adrian scare you?"

"No! No! He's a lovely man! It's just that he loves me SO much – he said he couldn't bear to lose me again, he said it would kill him……….and I believe him! Can you imagine the pressure that puts me under? I *can't* love him as much as he loves me – I *want* to, I *try* to, but…………..oh, God! I can't finish with him – he said it would kill him, I can't be responsible for that!"

There was an ominous silence at the table, suddenly broken by the arrival of two waiters , one carrying a large tray and the second waiter placing the food from the tray in front of each of them, and with a courteous "Enjoy your food, ladies" they both withdrew, leaving the girls looking at their plates as the impact of Abbi's last comment hung in the air.

"What do you want to do?" asked Carrie quietly, mixing the bolognaise sauce into her spaghetti.

There was silence for a few moments as Abbi picked up her knife and fork and rested both hands on the table. She took a deep breath in.

"There's nothing I can do. At least nothing that I can do that will change anything for the reasons I've explained. I'll just ……..carry on. Go with it. He's a good man, he'll look after me – he'd never hurt me. Although I don't love him as intensely as he loves me – that's not possible – I do care for him very deeply. We'll be comfortably happy together, we'll have a good life together. I mean, what else can a couple of sixty-odd year olds expect?"

"Well, I feel terrible about it all," said Carrie, "I mean, it was me who hunted him down, it was me who started this thing and now I feel like I've trapped you into a life you don't want!"

Abbi looked at her friend and was distressed to see tears in Carrie's eyes.

"No! No! You mustn't feel that way! Carrie, I asked you to find him – honestly, I became almost obsessed about finding him over the last couple of years! " said Abbi clutching at Carrie's hand while Noreen and Mel both agreed with Abbi's sentiment. "I suppose it was guilt that made me think so much about him – because of the way I treated him and as I've mellowed over the years, I wanted to put it right with him. I just didn't realise the impact I'd had on his life, and I suppose I was flattered when I did find out."

The women glanced at each other then back at Abbi as she gave a rueful smile. "I should have been more careful in what I wished for! Perhaps my long-lost love should have stayed as it was - a love long lost!"

*****

Missing Kate

The temperature inside the car had dropped. Lauren pulled her jacket closer and reached for her large woven tapestry bag, taking out a long, soft cashmere scarf that she wound round her neck. She placed her bag back on the passenger seat next to her and turned her gaze back to the sea. Between the low buildings ahead she could see the vast expanse of dark blue water as it stretched way out to meet the sky which had suddenly grown sullen with black storm clouds and the sea had darkened to match its mood and colour so that they both had turned a shade of indigo, becoming almost black and merging at the horizon. The sea-gulls wings flashed silver as they circled and swooped over the ocean and their sharp cries grated on her nerves like the constant yapping of a small dog.

Lauren needed to think and that was why she'd driven down to the coast. It was where she and Kate had always come to when they were younger and planning their future lives and where she needed to be on this day to try to clear the fog inside her head. It was a cold Sunday December morning and the place was deserted except for an occasional figure in the distance walking along the promenade wrapped up against the biting North wind. She'd had to park quite a distance away from the beach on one of the side streets as it was one of the few places that wasn't on a parking meter – chargeable even on a Sunday since the local authority's investment in the tourist industry, and she had no cash. She sighed deeply and opened the car door, reached into the back seat to get her thick woollen coat and when she was fully protected against the elements, she shrugged her bag onto her shoulder, locked the car and walked away heading towards the pier. She wanted to clear her head of the confusion and unhappiness that currently dwelt there and hoped the force of nature would do that. The wind was raw, blowing her hair madly around her head as it whipped and curled around her as she leaned into it to move forward. Once she reached the pier the wind became wilder, having no buildings or obstructions in its path. When she eventually arrived at the far end of the pier she looked out across the North Sea, absorbing the vastness and in comparison, feeling the smallness of herself and her problems. That's what she wanted – to put everything into perspective, to realise that whatever she decided, whatever she did, it didn't really matter – it would be so tiny, such a miniscule event it wouldn't even register in the Universe and the world would continue regardless.

She became aware of the tears on her cheeks but wasn't sure if they were caused by her emotions or by the icy wind. Her sadness had been part of her for so many months now that it was beginning to feel familiar, comfortable – like a pair of well-worn slippers. It was hard to remember what happiness felt like – she knew she *had* been happy at one time, but it felt long, long ago and at present she couldn't recall the feeling. She looked around and saw she was alone, the nearest figure some distance away on the beach. She turned to face the sea, took in a deep, deep breath, then screamed with all the force she could muster. It was a primal scream containing a pent-up ferocious rage, a burning frustration, deep grief and an intense heartache, and rose up from the depths of her inner being. The scream was so hard and so loud that she had to grab the rail to stop herself from falling to her knees and when her breath had expired she took in another lungful and screamed again, then a third time. The third scream caused her to stumble and almost fall to the ground. It had taken away all her strength and now she felt light-headed and hung on to the rail.

She turned away from the sea and stood with her back pushed against the railing for support. Exhaustion flooded her body and she stood limp and almost lifeless as her gaze flickered across the pier towards the promenade, seeing but not registering the coastal walkway, the fairground that stood idle, the summer chalets that stood vacant………….. and as her breathing became more controlled and her heartrate slowed, she grimaced. Her throat hurt with the force she'd used.

Her phone rang and she delved into her bag to bring it out, her heart sinking painfully as she saw Gerald's name on the screen. She stared at it till it stopped ringing, then a few seconds later a text notification from Gerald arrived. *"Where are you?"* She put her hand back into her coat pocket still clutching the phone while she thought about what she would say in reply. Then a minute later she brought it out and typed in, *"Shopping – won't be long."*

She didn't want to talk to him – she wasn't ready to face him because she knew it would lead to a confrontation and she was no match against him. She was playing for time, she needed more head space. She knew she was taking a chance when she left home this morning, but Gerald had gone for a pre-lunch game of squash at the Sports Club and she thought she'd be back before he came home. She sighed deeply and told herself there was no point in rushing back – 'might as well be hung for a sheep than a lamb' came unbidden into her head and at the moment she didn't care about anything.

She walked slowly along the promenade until she came to a sea-front café with a take-away kiosk. She noticed the sign which denoted credit cards accepted and her spirits lifted but soon plummeted when she realised the receipt would have the name and address of the company so Gerald would know where she'd been! This realisation seemed to epitomise her entire life with Gerald – she could spend whatever she wanted as long as it was within the confines of a credit card so that he could track every movement! She wanted to weep again and had to shake her head and take a deep breath in to be able to continue along the coastal path. She eventually came to a sturdy bench where she sat down and looked out again at the sea, relieved to find the dark sky was becoming lighter and the threat of rain was dissolving with the clouds, perhaps the winter sun may even break through.

She became aware that someone had sat down at the opposite end of the bench and she glanced towards the figure – a man, his coat collar turned up and his hands deep in his coat pockets. He glanced back at her and nodded briefly in acknowledgement then turned and stared out over the sea. They sat there for several minutes in silence, then he spoke.

"Makes you feel small, doesn't it?" he said.

She nodded and gave a small smile and turned her gaze back to the sea.

"Are you a visitor or do you live locally?" he asked.

"Local - about eight or nine miles away," she replied.

"I'm drawn to the sea, too," he continued, "Whenever I need to think about things – the view here has the effect of making my problems seem trivial, then I find I can face life again."

"Yes," she said, "That was why I came here today – to think!" She place an emphasis on the last word, knowing that she was being subtly dismissive towards him, but she wasn't in the mood for small talk - or any kind of talk – she wanted to continue with her thoughts.

"Sometimes you can overthink a situation," he mused, "Then it's counter-productive!"

"I suppose so," she said, "But how do you know you're over-thinking? Where's the cut-off point? What's the limit? How do I know I've reached the point where my thinking becomes over-thinking?" Her voice had tones of angry frustration in it.

"I don't know," he admitted, "I suppose when you keep going round in circles time after time, day after day, when you've been thinking and thinking and there doesn't seem to be a way forward!"

"In that case, I've spent most of my life overthinking!" said Lauren curtly.

"Sorry," he said with a small smile, "I'm not much help, am I?"

"Not really," she said turning away from him but then felt ill-mannered so she turned back and gave him a small smile in return. She shouldn't be so unpleasant towards him, he was trying to be helpful after all. He looked to be about thirty something – maybe early forties, with a mass of black hair - the style undetermined due to the wind blowing it vigorously, and very blue eyes. He had the current designer stubble that most men sported these days – *"Except Gerald"*, her inner voice said, *"He's always smooth and clean-shaven!"*

"I'm visiting," he said, changing the subject, "Came to spend the weekend with a pal from Uni days – he's just lost his wife, she was only thirty-six. So tragic!"

"Oh, I'm sorry to hear that," said Lauren, "That's very sad."

"Yeah," he looked out again towards the sea and Lauren could see the glint of tears in his eyes. "We were all at Uni together. She was lovely, such a clever girl as well – a Marine Biologist. He's a lecturer at Newcastle University. He's lost without her!" His voice had thickened with supressed emotion and Lauren felt a rush of pity for him. She was silent, not knowing what to say, her own emotions perilously near the surface so she turned to look out to the sea as well. They both sat there in deep contemplation for several minutes, then Lauren pulled her bag onto her shoulder and stood up.

"Well, I'd better be off," she said.

"Do you fancy a coffee," the man said suddenly. "I noticed a little café further down the promenade, "Please, just a coffee?"

Lauren hesitated. She really needed to get back home to make lunch. Then a rush of rebellion took her by surprise and she found herself saying, "Alright, just a coffee."

He stood up and put his hands in his pocket again, gesturing with his head the direction of the café which Lauren already knew as she had re-kindled her frustration against Gerald there twenty minutes or so previously. They walked side-by-side in comfortable silence till Lauren asked, "So where do you live then?"

"Just outside York," he replied, "Though I'm originally from Whitley Bay. I moved to York for my job - I'm a lecturer at the University."

They'd reached the café by this time and he moved forward to pull the door open and stood back to let her enter. She walked in, unwinding her scarf from round her neck and running her fingers through her windswept hair. He moved towards a table and held out a hand indicating to her to take a seat and he pulled out a chair opposite her and sat down. A waitress slowly approached and he looked up and said, "Two large coffees, please," then looking at Lauren he asked, "Do you want a cake – or sandwich, or anything?"

"No, thank you," she smiled, removing her leather gloves and putting them into her bag as the waitress turned and walked away.

"By the way, I'm Jonathan Gibson, - Jon," he said holding out his hand, and she replied, "Lauren Marston," as she shook his outstretched hand.

"So, at the risk of being told to mind my own business – what brought you here today?" he asked her.

"I …………just needed to think," she replied.

"Anything I can help you with?" he asked, "You know what they say – a problem shared……."

"Thank you, but I don't think anyone can help – I just have to make some decisions……." The waitress appeared just then and placed the coffees in front of them. "Thank you," said Lauren. Jon nodded and concentrated on putting sugar into his cup, stirring it slowly. Lauren took in a deep breath then as she exhaled she said, "I'm trying to decide whether or not to leave my husband!"

"I see," said Jon slowly as he took the spoon out of the cup and placed it on the saucer.

"I've not been happy for a long time………and my friend died suddenly ………..and I don't want to die feeling miserable! I want to be happy before I die!" she said in a rush.

Jon nodded. "That's not unreasonable," he said.

"I don't know why I married him!" she said shaking her head, then ran her fingers through her hair. "Yes, I do! It was infatuation, with him and his lifestyle …………and loneliness!"

"Loneliness?" he asked.

"Yes, stupid, I know! But I'd moved here with my job, left my family in Carlisle. I worked for Environmental Services and I met Gerald when I'd been here about nine or ten months. He's the Business Development Manager for the family's wine firm and I was homesick and lonely – I was working hard in the new job, found it hard to make friends and the flat I was in and the car repayments were taking most of my salary so I lived quite frugally. I'd reluctantly gone out to a Wine Bar with a group from work on a birthday do and he was there and we…………kind of hit it off. He flattered me, took me out to fabulous places and made me feel special."

Jon nodded again. "It figures," he said.

"We had a whirlwind courtship – he took me to places I'd only ever dreamed of. My parents thought he was wonderful – they were so happy that I'd found someone like him. They wanted me safely married same as my big sister and off their hands so that they could go travelling and enjoy their retirement with no responsibilities, so when he proposed one night in Paris – we'd flown there for the weekend – and I said yes, my mother started the wedding plans immediately and within twelve months of meeting him, I was married."

"So, when did it go wrong?" asked Jon gently.

"I don't know if it went ……….wrong…………it just never seemed………….right! Not really, if I think about it." Lauren screwed up her eyes. "It sounds bizarre, I know, but once I'd accepted his proposal I felt as if I was being pushed along, not in control, doing what was expected of me, playing the part – first as the dutiful daughter, then as the dutiful wife! I never questioned it , I just…………went along with everything. Then Kate………died……….." Lauren couldn't go on and she started to fidget with her hands that had been resting on the table. Jon carefully covered her hands with his and looked gently into her eyes.

"Was Kate the friend you mentioned?" he asked.

Lauren coughed to clear her throat. "Yes," she said almost in a whisper. "She was my oldest friend, my best friend. We'd grown up together, went to college together - then she went to live in Wales……. ironically to look after her mum when her dad died - her mum's got Parkinson's disease - and we'd meet up every other weekend, either I'd go down there or she'd come up here when she could get respite care for her mum. We'd talked about me getting a job in Wales and moving there near her, but I got this job – then soon afterwards I met Gerald…………..then, when I married Gerald I couldn't really fit it in - going there twice a month, so it became phone calls and text messages and visits once every three or four months………….. Nobody knew she was ill, until it was too late ……… She told me she had blurred vision – I told her to go to the optician………..it was a malignant brain tumour and she died within two weeks of diagnosis." The tears poured freely down Lauren's face and she pulled her hands free of Jon's and groped in her bag for a packet of tissues.

"I'm so sorry," said Jon, "That must have been incredibly hard for you."

"I never said goodbye," sobbed Lauren, "I didn't tell her how much she meant to me, I should have just gone – not cared about Gerald and ……………I should have put her first. But I didn't, I didn't know………… She was texting me, asking me how I was, not telling me she was dying…………..oh, God, she was dying but she didn't tell me!" She was crying uncontrollably now and Jon's eyes were moist as he empathised with her feelings.

The door opened and a woman and toddler came into the café, but neither Jon nor Lauren noticed. The waitress must have known them because she greeted them and carried on a conversation with the woman while the child clambered on a motorised but static elephant ride over by the door. Jon was silent as Lauren cried herself out, then when she had regained enough control to wipe her eyes and blow her nose, he squeezed her hands and said softly, "Feel better now? I guess you were needing that!"

"I'm so sorry," she said feeling embarrassed at her total melt-down.

"No, don't apologise," said Jon kindly, "You needed to let your grief out, I felt your pain, believe me!"

"Oh, I'm sorry, you've just lost your friend as well………." Lauren's face screwed up as if in some kind of agony, but Jon shook his head and said, "It helped me, your crying………… vicarious grieving!"

Lauren smiled ruefully, "You're very kind. I've not cried like that since she…………."

"So you definitely needed it," smiled Jon. They were both silent for several minutes, then Jon spoke.

"So where does your husband fit in here – why is your dilemma about whether you should leave him or not?"

"Because he doesn't make me happy - because I should have stood firm against him and gone down to Wales – I should have been with Kate when she died!" Lauren's voice had grown harsh and she picked at her fingernails.

Jon nodded slowly and hesitantly and decided to not push the conversation. He sat quietly, staring at his hands on the table in front of him and occasionally glancing at her to check her composure.

"I'd better go!" she said suddenly and started to gather her things together.

"Wait! No, don't go yet, please!" he beseeched her, "Have another coffee – just take a few more minutes till you're feeling better!" He had reached out his hand to place on top of hers and she stood still immediately, her gloves in one hand and her bag in the other. "Please, Lauren, just another coffee!"

"Okay," she said, "I must admit, I'm not ready to go back yet. This feels like………as if I was on holiday…….I suppose I *am* taking a vacation from my life! That little melt-down has purged me!" She gave a little chuckle and Jon smiled widely, his face lighting up at the sound of her laughter. He looked around and when the waitress saw him searching he beckoned for coffee refills and she smiled in compliance.

"Well, I've talked enough, it's your turn now, tell me about you," said Lauren settling back in the chair.

"Oh, nothing much to tell – I lead a very humdrum life! I've been teaching for the last seven years. I qualified when I was nearly twenty-four, then Sadie, Matt and I went travelling – supposed to be for a year, but it ended up nearly three years, then came home and eventually settled down into this job, though I spent a few years trying out different career paths. " He pursed his lips. "See, nothing much to tell!"

"I think the 'travelling for three years' bit belies that statement, it must have been a wonderful experience! Were Matt and Sadie……….."

Jon nodded. "Yes, they were the friends I told you about……..it was Sadie who died. They got married a year after we came back – were very happy together …………then she………….." His voice tapered off and he swallowed hard.

"You should take comfort in the fact that you have some wonderful memories of the three of you together," said Lauren softly and Jon nodded and smiled ruefully.

"Did you never marry?" asked Lauren, then they both fell silent as the waitress came and brought fresh coffees, taking away their used cups. When she'd gone, Lauren looked at him again, silently re-iterating the question with her eyes.

"Yes, I did, but it wasn't a success," he said quietly.

"I'm sorry," said Lauren, "Are you separated – or divorced?"

"We're not together……….though I haven't yet begun divorce proceedings. Actually, …………….she's in prison!" he said in a rush. "She stole from her employers – embezzled funds, 'cooked the books' as they say, and I knew nothing about it till they arrested her!"

"Oh, my!" said Lauren, feeling slightly uncomfortable at this revelation from a man she had just met, but then rationalised it by remembering an article she once read which said most disclosures take place in chance meetings – on a bus, in a queue, or like this one – on a coastal walk resting place and ending up in a café, and hadn't she just bared her soul to him just minutes before? "Well, I suppose you've got grounds for divorce," she added. "I haven't with Gerald, he hasn't actually done anything wrong!"

"I can't bring myself to file for divorce while she's locked away – it seems too harsh. She's due out soon, so we'll have to see. I think – going back to your situation …………..have you considered that you may be angry about your friend dying – which is a normal part of bereavement - and that's what has skewed your thinking and you're taking it out on your husband?" asked Jon softly.

"That's what he says when I try to talk to him – he dismisses my feelings and tells me to pull myself together and stop taking it out on him!" Her eyes had filled again and she fought to stay in control.

"Mmmmm! That's a bit harsh!" said Jon, "It's not easy to 'get over' someone you love dying as I know from my own experience!"

Lauren nodded. "Did you see Sadie before she died? Was hers sudden?"

Jon was silent for a few moments and looked to be wrestling with some inner turmoil, then he said, "She was killed in a car accident – a drunk driver was speeding on a country road and came round a blind corner on the wrong side of the road – straight into her. She was killed instantly! As he was, too, but I can't find any sympathy for him!"

"Oh, that's terrible!" said Lauren, aghast. "I mean, her dying, not you unable to find sympathy for the driver!"

He nodded. "So finding someone to throw my anger at is easy – but as he also died, it's impotent anger, and just stays inside………here!" He pressed his fist into his stomach as he said these words.

"What about her husband – Matt? How has he coped with it?" asked Lauren.

"Better than me, actually, but ………..it's complicated!" He shook his head and his face creased in pain as he wrestled again with his feelings and Lauren's heart went out to him as she had a sudden insight.

"Were you ………….in love with her?" she asked softly.

There was silence as Jon desperately tried to bring himself under control, then suddenly he moaned, "Yes, yes, I loved her! I'd loved her since I was seventeen, but she chose Matt!" He held his head in his hands with his elbows resting on the table. "I thought I'd be okay with it, we were all such good friends, we went everywhere together – I know she cared about me – but she loved Matt…….she loved him the way I loved her………And now she's gone!"

They sat in silence. Lauren had placed her hands over his hand that was on the table and her heart ached with a misery she was all too familiar with. Neither of them had noticed the café filling up with customers nor the sound level rising as they were both lost in their own sorrow and anguish. After a few minutes, Jon took in a deep breath. "I've never verbalised that before! I've lived with it for so long but have never put it into words out loud. It's strange, but I feel as if a weight has been lifted from me. Thank you."

Lauren couldn't speak, her throat was so tight she could barely even breathe. She smiled feebly at him and blinked back tears, then took her hands away from his and as she felt a vibration from her pocket, she drew out her phone out. She glanced at the screen then gasped. Seven missed calls and three text messages – all from Gerald! She had flicked the phone onto silent when she'd sent the first text message telling him she was shopping and wouldn't be long. The text messages all read the same – *Where are you?* and the last one was in shouty capitals!

"I'd better go – I'm in big trouble now!" she said, standing up and gathering her things together.

"Can we keep in touch? Please? No hidden agenda or anything, but I feel that we have a connection - I can talk to you and hope you can talk to me – we could do some co-counselling ………….." He was talking quickly trying to get the words out before she dashed out of the door. He had groped in his pocket to bring his wallet out and took out a business card, thrusting it at her saying, "Please, just send me a text – or an email to let me know how you get on – that's all, no strings attached, just friends. We can help each other!" He threw a ten-pound note onto the table to cover the cost of the coffees and followed her to the door, calling "Thank you!" to the waitress as he quickly pursued Lauren outside. She stopped and turned to him.

"Thank you very much for the coffees and for listening to me." She looked down at the card in her hand and smiled at him. "Yes, Dr Jonathan Gibson, I will text you – I can't email as we don't have the internet …………..Gerald won't have it installed and he won't allow social media."

"Oh? That's a shame, but I'm sure we can work round it, just keep my number and send me a text……please?" He smiled at her and stepped forward, aiming to kiss her on the cheek, but she had also taken a step towards him so their bodies collided. She caught the aroma of his after-shave mingled with fresh, salty sea air and felt herself melt into him as his arms came around her instinctively. She felt a rush of warm comfort, a feeling of security – a safeness that she hadn't known was lacking until she felt it with him at that moment and then it became an aching void when their bodies drew apart.

An hour or so later as her car drew up outside the front door and Lauren's feet alighted on the gravelled drive, Gerald appeared at the door.

"Where the hell have you been?" he shouted, "You know we've got people coming this evening ……………and you haven't even made lunch!"

"Sorry……..sorry……….I forgot……….I'll do it now!" stuttered Lauren as she hastily grabbed her bag and closed the car door. All the boldness and courage she'd felt previously dissolved within seconds.

"Where's your shopping?" demanded Gerald and as she gave him a blank look he snapped, "Your shopping – you said you were shopping when I messaged you! Where is it?"

"Oh………I didn't buy anything," she replied, colour creeping into her cheeks.

"So, all that time……..'shopping'……….and you come away empty-handed!" Gerald tutted loudly and marched past her into the entrance hall. She meekly followed behind him and made to go into the kitchen, but his voice stopped her.

"Don't bother making any lunch – it's too late now! I made do with a sandwich from some chicken that was in the fridge. You need to get into the kitchen and start getting organised! The caterers will be here any minute and the food is arriving at three-thirty – and leave enough time to get yourself sorted – you look a mess! What the hell have you been doing?"

He marched away without waiting for an answer and Lauren turned and made her way into the kitchen, her heart heavy as the familiar despondency settled around her like a cloak. Another nerve-wracking, ostentatious evening with Gerald's so-called 'friends' – the kind of people that Lauren at one time had been delighted to spend time with, but who now bored her to death with their pretentiousness and their shallow-mindedness. There was nothing genuine about any of them – Barbara Bailey was a first-class snob and her husband Desmond made Lauren's flesh crawl with his red blotchy face which was always covered in a sheen of perspiration and his fat, podgy fingers that constantly seemed to 'accidently' touch her every time she went past him. The Bensons were no better – Hilary Benson was the Secretary at the Golf Club and couldn't understand Lauren's reluctance to take up golf as a hobby – or 'way of life' as she saw it, and her husband

Charles who was also an avid golfer and a landowner with a nine-bedroomed country house that had been in his family for several generations. The other four couples making up the guest list were James and Suzanna Gilroy and George and Megan Davenport, both restaurateurs and potential new customers and Sam and Jenny Boothroyd and Oscar and Harriet Whitfield. Lauren had never met them before, but every time Gerald arranged a dinner-party there would be some new people there whom he wanted to impress and hopefully get business from and he used the Baileys and the Bensons as an indication of his success in life!

But they were all important business clients so Lauren's role was to flatter and sweet-talk them all – particularly the men as it was them that usually brought in the custom - expensive wines not only for their own abundant use but also because of their influences in the business world, and the women - who were 'prominent in female circles' according to Gerald - and that was important for her social standing and ultimately Gerald's father's business.

When she had first married Gerald she was aware of his drive and ambition and it added to the attraction, so the many business trips abroad he always seemed to be making added to the glamour as she very often accompanied him. Lauren had been swept along with this lifestyle, unaccustomed as she was to prosperity and mingling with such wealthy business clients and she had basked in the luxury of hosting fabulous dinner parties where staff were employed to cook, wait and serve and all she needed to do was look elegant and make small talk.

Then Kate died and everything changed. The pain of loss hit her again in the middle of her chest. The intensity hadn't decreased since the day she died – the day that Kate's mum Sarah had phoned to tell her, her voice quivering and the sobs wracking her, telling her that her best friend was dead! She couldn't take it in – Kate had only been diagnosed two weeks previously with a brain tumour – but Kate had assured her that tumours these days weren't such a threat and could be shrunk with radio-therapy. It was only at the funeral when Lauren sensitively questioned Sarah that she discovered that Kate knew she would die and wanted to shield Lauren. She hadn't received any treatment – she knew it wouldn't help, the tumour was too large and aggressive, so she spent the last few days that she was able to walk and talk going round visiting Nursing Homes to ensure that her mum would be taken care of after she'd gone.

Lauren dragged her thoughts back to the present as a knock on the garden door alerted her to the arrival of the caterers and she hastily ran her fingers through her hair, suddenly aware of her windswept and rather unkempt appearance. Fortunately, the chef was Robert and his assistants and waiting-on staff were people that had been there before for previous functions, so Lauren smiled in acknowledgement and relief as Robert had always in the past produced exquisite meals and the assistants were familiar with the kitchen and dining-room so Lauren didn't have to spend too much time showing them where everything was. She informed Robert that the food was arriving at any moment – Gerald had previously gone through the menu with him over the phone so Lauren could order whatever Robert would need to produce his masterpieces - then she ended by saying that Gerald would be in shortly to go through the wines once more when the sommelier had arrived. For obvious reasons the wines were integral to the success of the evening and Gerald, acting on the advice of his sommelier, insisted on certain foods to accompany the evening's wines so it was vitally important that nothing on the menu would taint the palette.

After Lauren had signed for the arrival of the food and was assured by Robert that everything would run smoothly, she left the kitchen. A last glance in through the dining-room door as she walked past reassured her that everything was in place as a young girl, smartly attired in black uniform and pristine white apron with her short, dark hair tidily tucked into a white cap expertly flicked the huge white tablecloth across the large oak table, smoothing it out as she swiftly walked around it then moved over to the sideboard that contained the cutlery, the place settings and table centre-pieces. Lauren left her to it and walked to the base of the large wide staircase that tapered as it circled round to the upper floor, walking slowly up the stairs, feeling the weight of her melancholy and wishing that it would shift to allow her some relief.

As she reached the bedroom the door pulled open and Gerald strode out.

"Is Robert and his staff here?" he demanded and she nodded. "Good! I'm just going to sort the wines out – you get yourself sorted!" he snapped. He leaned across and took her face in his hand, pinching her chin as he scrutinised her. "You know how important this dinner is – make sure you're in top form!" Then he kissed her roughly and aggressively on the lips and abruptly turned away, striding down the corridor and bounding down the stairs.

She dragged the back of her hand across her mouth with a shudder and went into the bedroom. She sank down on the bed and sighed deeply trying to muster up some energy or enthusiasm. Was it only three hours ago that she was sitting in the sea-side café pouring her heart out to Jon, a man she had just met, a stranger, but who already felt like she had known forever. She took his card from her jacket pocket and looked at it. She mustn't let Gerald find it! She looked guiltily around her, then taking out her phone she copied his details under the name 'Jan' Gibson then tore up the card into tiny pieces and put them in the bin by her dressing table, pushing the pieces down under the cotton-wool and tissues. As a final act of defiance, she hastily typed, "Hi, thanks for the chat today. Lauren" and before she could change her mind she pressed 'send' and off the message flew.

She filled the bath, pouring in bath crème and perfumed oils then quickly ran down the stairs to collect a bottle of wine and a wine glass from the dining-room dresser, then just as speedily ran back upstairs before Gerald had a chance to spot her. She wouldn't be able to relax without the help of a glass of wine, and as she lay back in the warmth of the scented water she tried to imagine what her life would have been like if she'd married someone else ……… say…………..a college lecturer……….. or a University professor? She felt her muscles ease and her mind become calmer as the wine was absorbed into her body and she hazily remembered that she'd had no lunch – nothing to eat since breakfast.

She pictured herself hand-in-hand with someone walking along the promenade, laughing at funny things he said, her hair blowing wildly in the wind - and knew beyond doubt that Gerald would never fit in that picture! Then she imagined them camping in a two-man tent – the way that she and Kate had done many, many times, eating fish and chips out of paper wrappings as they sat cross-legged in front of a tiny camp-fire, wearing track suits and trainers and bobble-hats for warmth. Ah, yes, she was happy then. She and Kate used to laugh so much - even when the rain was pouring down and they were soaked, they still laughed. She grimaced ruefully. That was the life she had willingly waved goodbye to when Gerald came along brandishing his bank cards and wealthy life-style. Gerald had promised her excitement, travel, dinner-parties – he'd told her she was an asset to his business because of her beauty and he showered her with gifts and jewellery, then followed it up with several expensive dresses for her to attend his functions, manicures, high class hair salons, telling her she was an investment. She loved it!

When Kate had moved down to Wales to look after her mum Lauren missed her terribly, even more so when she moved with the new job. She rang her several times a week at first, then told her about this rich guy she had met and they giggled together as Lauren excitedly told her about the places they went, the restaurants they frequented – she sent her photos of the gowns and dresses he'd bought for her to attend the dinner-parties and functions and all she had to do was to look beautiful and mildly flirt with Gerald's business associates while hanging on to his arm. After a while Kate didn't giggle so much and Lauren's excited boasting was sometimes met with uncomfortable silences. On her next trip to Wales as they sat curled up on the sofa after Kate's mum was safely tucked up in bed, Lauren confronted her and asked her what was wrong and Kate asked her gently if that was really the life she wanted for herself.

"How could I not want this lifestyle?" she'd replied, slightly ruffled at Kate's question. "He obviously loves me and would do anything for me. He's handsome, he's rich and his parents like me, he says I'm good for the business………….Aw, Kate! I want you to be happy for me!"

"If you're happy, then I'm happy!" Kate had replied, "It's just so different from what we're used to."

"Exactly!" exclaimed Lauren, "I'd be a fool to let this one go!"

It hadn't taken her long to get used to this new lifestyle. Lauren's own parents were over the moon to find she had snared such a good catch in comparison to her older sister who had married the boy she had dated since high school and although they were blissfully happy, he wasn't in a high salaried position and within five years of being married they had two children to raise. The children were now five and eight years old and in full-time school so now Beth had taken part-time work in a local hairdressing salon. Beth and Lauren met up a couple of times a month for lunch - Lauren had invited them in the early days to their home but Beth felt uncomfortable in Gerald's company and he completely ignored the children who were Beth and Michael's pride and joy and so she had made excuses each time Lauren invited her after that. Soon Lauren stopped inviting her and they were both satisfied with occasionally meeting up in town for lunch or afternoon tea, which fortunately Lauren insisted on paying for – Beth couldn't afford to eat out frequently on the salary that Michael brought home and her wage from the salon was small. On very rare occasions Beth would bring the children to see Lauren on a Sunday when Gerald was away on business and Lauren hadn't gone with him.

When Lauren had married Gerald, her parents had sold the family home and downsized into a small but very modern bungalow with the intention of using their savings to enjoy their retirement, holidaying round the world. Which they were doing – at present on an extended Mediterranean cruise. Lauren wasn't surprised at her parent's actions – all the while she and Beth were growing up they had said their intention was to see their girls married and settled, then they were off. They visited when they were back in England and kept in touch by email and messaging on social media to Beth while they were away, posting photographs of their holiday destinations which Beth showed to Lauren when they met up so they weren't worried about them, but deep down Lauren felt a sense of abandonment as their departure came so soon after her marriage.

When Lauren had secured the job in Environmental Services, she thought she was in a job with a career ahead of her – she had started in a junior position, but the prospects were good and her father had drummed it into her as she was growing up to get a position with a good work's pension – and what was better than the Local Authority? But her living expenses took up most of her income – the rent on the flat was high, but the properties with low rents were in less salubrious areas. She could only afford an occasional night out because she put all her spare cash into travelling to Wales to see Kate and her mum. So when Gerald entered her life it was as if he'd come to save her from her penny-pinching existence.

The sudden realisation that she was lying in a bathtub of lukewarm water brought her back to the present. She hastily clambered out and wrapped herself in a huge, fluffy bath sheet, coiling her wet hair and winding a towel turban-style round her head. She picked up her wine-glass and the bottle and walked into the bedroom. She was really hungry now and feeling slightly light-headed from the wine, but she felt calm and relaxed enough to face the evening. She daren't go into the kitchen to get some food as she knew Robert would be very busy, preparing, cooking and issuing orders to his assistants and she didn't want to get in their way. Or bump into Gerald.

She poured another glass of wine and took a seat at her dressing-table. She regarded her image in the mirror dispassionately, noting the tiny lines at the corner of her eyes but otherwise a flawless complexion. This could be due to the many facials and spa treatments she had received – she didn't go out to work so she spent her time lunching with the wives of Gerald's business associates, or shopping, or attending manicures and hairdressing appointments and when Gerald went abroad on business and she went with him she would spend the days in luxury Spa and Wellness Centres. It was important that she maintained her good looks, as Gerald often reminded her - that was her only contribution to the business. She had good bone structure – high cheekbones and a smooth forehead. She turned her head slowly from side to side examining herself from every angle. If there was a flaw…….. Gerald would spot it!

She carefully applied her make-up making sure that there were no uneven shades or textures. Gerald insisted that she looked professionally made-up and not painted and had paid for her to attend expensive cosmetic seminars where she was taught how to apply make-up professionally. Fortunately, her hair was shoulder-length and golden blonde with a gentle natural curl that took minimal effort to look shining and beautiful. Her hair was the feature that Gerald prized the most and he loved to run his fingers through it – much to her annoyance when she was trying to remain composed and elegant.

She had just slipped into her dress – a short, Rebecca Valance emerald-green fitted number with a low-cut neckline that revealed her ample bosoms without making her look indecent, when Gerald walked into the room.

"Are you nearly ready?" he barked, and as she nodded silently and turned to pick up her short bolero jacket to slip onto her shoulders, he grabbed her by the arm and turned her to face him.

"I want to know exactly where you were today!" he hissed. "You weren't shopping – you weren't dressed for it! You would never have shown yourself in public looking the way you did! So, when everyone has gone tonight – I want some answers!" He spun on his heel and strode to the door, pulled it open and went out, slamming it behind him.

Lauren swallowed nervously. Tonight was going to be a nightmare! He would be watching her every move and taking every opportunity to hurl veiled criticisms at her that only she would get the gist of. She felt a rush of tears again and fought furiously to blink them back in – she couldn't afford the time to redo her make-up, nor could she afford to show her vulnerability! Once he spied a weakness, he would plunge the knife in. She needed more wine! She stumbled to her dressing-table and poured out the last of the bottle into her wine-glass, gulping it down swiftly and feeling the cracks seal up. Her armour was back in place! She slipped on her green Jimmy Choo shoes, smoothed her dress over her hips and purposefully straightening her back, she opened the bedroom door and made her way down the staircase.

The evening was a success, due mainly to the skill and knowledge of the sommelier that Gerald always brought in to heighten the lavishness and impressiveness of the dinner party. As he slowly and casually made his way around the table with his *tastevin* – the small, silver wine-tasting cup subtly encouraging everyone to taste the wines that Gerald wished to promote that evening and giving lengthy explanations about each of the vineyards and the wine-making process, Lauren was doing what Gerald had trained her for, coyly flirting with the businessmen and demurely flattering the influential wives By the time the dinner party was at an end, Gerald had secured quite a substantial amount of business.

When everyone had gone, Lauren went into the kitchen for a glass of water to take up to bed. She looked around in wonder and admiration at the immaculate condition the kitchen had been left in – Robert always made sure that his staff left no traces of their presence. Lauren shook her head in amazement to think that a few hours previously, this kitchen had produced such an array of dishes that drew compliments from every person present at the party. Every working surface had been covered as Robert and his commis chef worked speedily and efficiently and the kitchen assistant washed up and cleaned surfaces as they were needed, while the two waitresses saw to the place settings and servings. At the end of the evening everyone helped to clean – including Robert, who oversaw the whole procedure.

She filled her glass and walked quickly up the stairs. Gerald had gone into his office to draw up the paperwork for the orders he had secured so that he could email the copies first thing next morning when he got to work before anyone had time for second thoughts. Once she was in her bedroom, she hastily undressed and began to clean her make-up off, hoping to be in bed before he came up, therefore delaying the interrogation he had threatened her with earlier that evening. Her heart sank as she heard the door open and she turned to him with what she hoped was a seductive smile.

"I think everyone enjoyed themselves this evening – Hilary certainly did!" she said brightly.

"Yes, I believe so," he replied, "We did well. I liked the way you steered the conversation away from the golf course when Charles got on his high horse ………very clever," he said ponderingly. Lauren felt her shoulders relax slightly and dared to think he had forgotten his earlier warning.

"Have you made any lunch dates?" he asked.

"Yes," she replied, "It had to be after Christmas, everyone had full diaries – it's eighteenth of January, that's the Thursday after we come back from Italy, at *Sylvanie's* with Suzanna Gilroy and Megan Davenport, the wives of……………….

"Is it in the diary?" he interjected. There was a large desk diary in his office where she always had to write down her appointments and every evening before retiring for bed she had to check the diary for the next day's schedule so if he asked her where she was going to be at a particular time, she could tell him. This even applied to shopping, or days out with her sister and included visits from either set of parents – everything was logged in the diary.

She nodded and turned back to the mirror and continued cleaning her face.

"I noticed that there was nothing in the diary for this morning………….yet you were out when I came home! And, you said you were shopping yet brought nothing home!" As he spoke he was concentrating on folding his trousers.

Lauren's heart began to hammer in her rib-cage. "I….…..er….…..I went for a little drive ……………to the coast," she blustered.

"Any particular reason why you didn't put it in the diary?" he said icily.

"I didn't think……I thought I wouldn't be long……I didn't think it was important," she faltered.

He sighed deeply and put his hands on her shoulders, looking intently at her through the mirror on her dressing-table. His eyes were like steel and he spoke slowly and in a clipped, even tone.

"How many times do I have to tell you – EVERYTHING goes in the diary! I need to know where you are ALL THE TIME! I do NOT want to come home again and find nothing in the diary and you not in the house! Is that clear? Do you understand?" His voice was rising and his face had lost colour. Lauren could almost feel the anger that emanated from him. "Now you've made me suspicious – why did you sneak out? Why tell me you were shopping when I first asked you? And why would you lie to me if you're not doing something you shouldn't be doing? Why not just say you'd been for a drive? Can you understand, Lauren, can you see how a simple instruction that is not followed can create such controversy?" As he spoke his fingers were digging into her shoulders to give emphasis to his words.

She felt the tears dart to her eyes. "I'm sorry," she whispered, "I was feeling sad.........I was missing Kate........."

He dropped his hands from her shoulders and stepped backwards, his eyes raised to the ceiling. "Here we go again!" he said in exasperation, "Missing Kate...........again! Isn't it about time you moved on from this? I know she was your long-time friend, but for goodness sake, Lauren, you hardly saw her since we got married!"

"I know!" she cried, "And that's what hurts me! I hardly saw her – I wasn't there for her...........she was ill and dying and I wasn't there for her!" Tears were pouring down her face now and she covered her face with her hands. Gerald had once told her that she was an ugly crier so she always hid her face when she cried.

He batted his hand on his forehead. "For God's sake, Lauren, pull yourself together! You're a married woman with responsibilities! You can't just drop everything in your life and go and sit with an ailing friend, even if she WAS dying! It wouldn't have saved her! She would STILL have died!" He was pacing the bedroom floor, shaking his head in disbelief. "As my wife, you have a position to uphold! We have a very successful business in which we all have to play our part! If you want to play nursemaid every time one of your friends gets ill…………at least PUT IT IN THE BLOODY DIARY! Then I can work round it!" He stormed out of the room leaving her sobbing at her dressing-table, her head still in her hands.

After a few moments when her sobbing had reduced to a snivel, she raised her head and looked at her face in the mirror. Gerald was right – she looked a mess! Her face was blotchy and her eyes were puffed and red! She stared at her reflection. How could Gerald be so cruel? He knew how Kate's death had shocked her. He had been caring and comforting when it happened, but when she came back from the funeral – he didn't go as he had an important business meeting that he couldn't miss – he expected her to be back to normal, carrying out her duties when all she wanted to do was to curl up in a corner and sob. He became impatient with her, walking out of the room if she suddenly started to cry – which happened a lot at first. Now, three months later, if she mentioned Kate's death he became angry.

Jon wouldn't behave like that, she thought – *he would let me cry, even hold me while I did so. It's Gerald who is wrong – he has no feelings! He's never lost anyone, he doesn't know what bereavement feels like! One day he will – he'll lose someone – his mother or father and he'll understand what the pain is like!*

She got up slowly and went towards the bed and crawled under the covers. She wanted to be asleep when he came back into the room – he would be sitting in his office drinking his expensive whisky and gloating over the business he had pulled in tonight. That's what was important to him – showing his father how successful he was, always trying to please him, always looking for his approval but never quite achieving it. His older brother, Nathan, was doing missionary work in Africa since he had been disowned by his father, and his mother Marjorie obeyed her husband so she hadn't seen her son for over twenty years. Nathan was his father's pride and joy until drugs had robbed him of his health and self-respect and he was stealing vast sums of money from the business to fund his cocaine addiction. When George had found out about his son's habit and the damage he had wreaked on the business, he forced him into a Rehab Centre and refused any contact with him. He cut him off entirely and when Nathan was eventually clean, he tried to visit his parents but his father refused point blank to have anything to do with him and ordered his wife to ignore him too. Gerald was twelve years younger than Nathan so was just a boy of eleven when this occurred with Nathan, so he didn't really understand what had happened, he just knew he had an older brother that he hadn't seen for the past twenty-three years.

Lauren's eyes had become droopy as these thoughts had whirled round and round her head and she snuggled under the duvet. George Marston was a force to be reckoned with and she was completely intimidated by him. Marjorie was a gentle soul who complied with every demand that her husband made. As she drifted into sleep, her final thoughts were, *Is this my future – am I the Marjorie Marston of the next generation? Is that what I really want?*

As soon as Lauren awoke the next morning she remembered about sending Jon a text message. She hadn't dared to look at her phone while Gerald was around in case he saw her and wanted to know who she was in contact with. She had found in the past that telling fibs or not being completely truthful to him when he asked her something caused untold misery, as yesterday's innocent trip to the beach confirmed. Gerald had left the house as she realised when she looked out of the window and saw his car wasn't on the drive and the garage door was raised – he left it that way so he could drive straight into it when he came home. He hadn't come to bed the night before – or so she guessed by the untouched duvet on his side of the bed, but that was no surprise – he often slept on the large sofa in his office when he got into a rage and drank too much whisky.

Wrapping herself in a satin robe, she went to her dressing table drawer where she had put her phone the night before when she had sent the text message to Jon. Her heart skipped a beat when she saw she had a message and she quickly opened it. It read *Hi Lauren, good to hear from you. I enjoyed our chat. Is there any chance I could ring you – for longer chats? Obviously, when it's convenient – I don't want to cause trouble for you.* She held the phone to her chest, a small smile on her lips. He meant it, then, – about really talking, expressing things that would normally be kept locked away. They had a shared heartache, both losing a friend they loved – though he had loved Sadie as more than a friend. Being able to talk would be more sensible, they could say more than a text message could. She had ripped up his business card yesterday once she had stored his number as Jan Gibson.

She needed to think of whether there was any way that Gerald would find out that she was in contact with someone that he didn't know. She had very few friends left from her life before he came into it – almost all of her acquaintances now were associated with his business or his squash club. She went downstairs into the kitchen and poured herself some juice while she thought about it from every angle As long as she made sure to delete each text message after she'd sent it – he sometimes scrolled through her messages to see whether she had made any appointments and not entered them into the diary, but more importantly to delete her call history – though if the records showed 'Jan Gibson' it would appear innocuous enough. Perhaps she'd better start talking casually about someone called Jan – it could be someone she met in the beauty parlour or at the hairdresser. Gerald probably wouldn't take any notice of chit-chat like that – he was only interested in her life as part of the business, idle gossip went over his head.

Oh, why does it have to be like this? she cried inwardly, *Why can't Gerald be the kind and considerate man I thought he was when we first met? When did he become this cruel tyrant – why did I not notice what was happening?* He had been such an attentive boyfriend, had completely swept her off her feet and she was besotted with him and his lifestyle. He used to stare at her in awe, telling her she was the most beautiful woman on earth and as Lauren was completely unused to being admired so openly, his words made her feel confident and desirable and this was reflected in her strikingly blue eyes that gleamed and sparkled and made her skin look radiant and therefore even more beautiful. Gerald himself was an extremely handsome man, tall and athletic with blond wavy hair and electric-blue eyes, but these eyes could glitter like shards of glass when he was angry and his full lips would pull into a thin line making him look cruel and ruthless.

She hadn't notice the transformation - it was so gradual and subtle and she constantly made excuses for him. His father, George Marston, was similar in character. George was a hard-nosed business-man but in his presence Gerald was quite meek and submissive, but George intimidated Lauren without even trying, so she didn't expect Gerald to be anything other than compliant. She noticed that they never mentioned Nathen – and she daren't raise the topic, even when she and Marjorie were alone. Gerald had told her that his father had disowned him and refused to have his name mentioned in his house.

When Kate died, Lauren's parents were abroad and couldn't get back for the funeral – though Lauren thought that they probably could if they had made the effort, and she found this hard to forgive in them. She felt as though they had withdrawn their responsibility and support towards her when she got married as they excitedly took up their own independent lives. Her sister Beth had gone with her to Wales to pay her respects and to say her own goodbye to her sister's best friend that she had known for as long as Lauren had, though obviously not as intensely. Beth had been Lauren's emotional prop for a couple of weeks following the funeral, but Lauren realised that Beth had her own family to care for and didn't think it was fair to burden Beth with her grief. After all, Lauren had her own husband who should be taking care of his wife in her distressed state – but unfortunately he didn't do that!

She was meeting Beth today for lunch – the date had been in the diary for a couple of weeks now, ever since they last met. She tried to meet with Beth as often as she could, but Beth had a busy life with two children and a husband to care for as well as her part-time job. Lauren was looking forward to meeting up with Beth and while she buttered some toast and poured coffee she thought about confiding in Beth about meeting Jon the day before. This made her think about him – how attentive he had been about how she felt, as though her feelings were important. This thought pulled her up sharply – of course her feelings were important! It was Gerald who dismissed them – meeting Jon and being listened to by him had put Gerald under the spotlight and showed how he was lacking in so many areas. She knew that she would be happier without him, but she had grown to be comfortable in this luxurious life-style – could she really go back to scrimping and saving, living from one payday to the next? She looked around the kitchen – it was probably the size of the whole apartment she had left when she married Gerald!

She took a deep breath and exhaled slowly. Perhaps she should talk to Beth about how disastrous she felt her marriage now was. She knew Beth would be upset, but that would be because Lauren was unhappy, whereas her parents would be upset that she was giving up on a secure marriage. She could hear her mother's voice in her head, telling her that all marriages had to be worked on, that nothing just happened without putting effort in and she hadn't given it long enough to just walk away. Her father would sigh in exasperation and tell her to grow up and take her share of the responsibility for their relationship – it was a partnership and all partnerships hit bad patches and you just had to work through them. *Not much support there, then,* she thought to herself with a sinking heart.

She walked round the house inspecting to make sure everything was in its place – Gerald had high standards that she was expected to maintain in the house, then she took the food out of the freezer to defrost for that evening's meal. Gerald would be home for dinner as there was nothing in the diary for that evening – he often had evening meetings when he would dine out so she would eat alone. Once she was sure that the house was in near-perfect condition she ran upstairs to get showered and dressed.

On her way to meet Beth, she deliberately turned her mind away from her current problems and focused on listening to a radio chat show. She was meeting her sister in Gateshead's Intu Metrocentre – one of Europe's largest indoor mall-style shopping centres about an hour's drive away - as they had arranged that Lauren would buy the girls their Christmas presents and Beth could take them home with her after Lauren had them gift-wrapped as she and Gerald were going to Italy for Christmas. Beth was travelling in on a bus as she had no car and the Metrocentre had its own bus service that would bring her right into the Centre. Lauren would park up in the car park nearest where Beth would get off the bus then ring Beth and they would co-ordinate their positions till they met up.

It worked well and they waved at each other as they both approached the designated coffee shop at the same time. Lauren hugged her sister with perhaps more feeling than she had in the past as she felt she really needed to feel loved and wanted by someone at this present time.

"Hi, sweetie, you okay?" asked Beth as she felt the extra intensity of Lauren's embrace.

"I'm glad to see you – I've missed my big sister!" said Lauren, lightening the statement with a laugh, but definitely meaning the words.

"Anything wrong?" asked Beth with a worried frown as she took Lauren's arm in hers and they turned towards the coffee-shop.

"No, I'm fine," said Lauren, "Do you want a coffee or shall we go straight for lunch?"

"We might as well go straight for lunch if we want to do some shopping as well – I only have until three o'clock – the girls are in an after-school crafts club till four, so I need to get the bus back at ten past three."

They walked to the huge information board that displayed the position of each of the shops and restaurants and selected where they would eat, then where they would go to buy the girl's Christmas presents. Once that was decided, they set off to the restaurant arm-in-arm and Beth told her how the girls were doing at school, how her own job was working out and how Michael had been given promotion at work which meant a salary increase. She excitedly told her how they were planning on having some work done on the house next March – a conservatory at the back and a garden revamp. Beth's eyes were shining as she described what they had planned and Lauren smiled and squeezed her sister's hand, feeling really happy for her.

They reached the small Italian restaurant that they had chosen and as they were shown to their seats by a tall, dark, handsome waiter Lauren had a sickening thought flash through her mind - *I'll have to give up lunching like this if I leave Gerald!* Then just as quickly she told herself that Beth didn't have this lifestyle and look how happy she was.

"It's my treat, so order whatever you fancy – it's our Christmas celebration meal, so let's push the boat out!" said Lauren and squeezed her sister's hand.

Lauren ordered a glass each of an expensive Merlot to sip while they perused the menu and they finally settled on stuffed mushrooms for starters, followed by *Agnelli* - pan-fried rack of lamb with potatoes and vegetables of the day, and ending with tiramisu for Lauren and profiteroles for Beth. They settled back in the comfortable leather chairs and Beth asked Lauren how things were going with Gerald's father's business.

"Oh, it's fine. Gerald's brought in a lot of new contracts in the last couple of weeks – we had a dinner party last night that netted some good business. He works very hard." Lauren was forcing a smile on her face and enthusiasm into her voice and even to herself it sounded strained, but Beth didn't seem to notice.

Lauren leaned forward and with her elbows on the table she steepled her fingers. "Beth, I……..err…….." She took a deep breath in and Beth leaned towards her expecting Lauren to divulge a confidence or worry but then Lauren exhaled slowly and dropped her gaze then said, " I don't know what to get for the girls. Have you any ideas??"

Beth looked slightly taken aback, fully expecting Lauren to disclose something, but she recovered well and said, "Well,

Claire would like one of those American fashion dolls – she's into clothes and fashion already, whereas Rachel would love a fairy castle with a couple of fairies, bless her, she's still my baby!" They both laughed and Lauren said, "Ah, that's great – I honestly never know where to start when trying to choose something for them – I know nothing about children!"

"No signs of you and Gerald starting a family?" asked Beth taking a sip of her wine.

"God! No!" said Lauren emphatically, then as she saw Beth's eyebrows raise she quickly added, "He's always busy, I'd have to raise the child on my own! Besides, I'm not ready yet."

"Well, don't leave it too long," said Beth, "You're going to be thirty next birthday!"

"Don't remind me!" said Lauren in mock horror.

Just then the food arrived and so the conversation was halted and then took a different turn as Beth entertained Lauren by describing some of the antics that her children got up to and they laughed and giggled as they remembered some of the similar frolics that they themselves had performed. They talked about their parents and Beth showed Lauren the latest photos they had sent via social media and Lauren had to admit that they both look extremely well and happy. She had confessed to Beth when they were in Wales for Kate's funeral that she felt abandoned by her parents and Beth had hugged her and said that her parents knew that she would look after her little sister and that Beth would always be there for her, no matter what.

After a while, slowly sipping coffee, Beth looked at her watch and said, "Gosh, look at the time – we'd better go if we want to get these gifts for the girls."

Lauren gestured for the waiter to bring the bill and took her credit card out of her phone wallet..

"I don't have a purse now," she told Beth, "There's no point – I never have any cash, everything is by card."

The waiter brought the bill and Lauren handed him the card without even looking at the bill. A few minutes later the waiter came back with a very apologetic look on his face.

"I am very sorry, Madame," he said in faltering English, "But our card machine is not working – we have troubles with our connections. Is it possible that you can pay with cash?"

"No!" said Lauren, shaking her head, "I don't use cash! You must have some other option."

"Madame, if you will bear with us, I will have to ring your bank for clearance for the card – can you please wait? I am so very sorry!"

"Look, I'll pay," said Beth taking out her purse, "We don't have time to wait. Where's the bill?" The waiter handed her the small silver salver with the bill on it and returned Lauren's card to her. She saw Beth's eyes widen as she saw the amount and taking a deep breath she counted out seventy pounds and placed it on the salver, then turned as another waiter brought their coats and silently slid her hands into the sleeves as the waiter, smiling obsequiously, smoothed the jacket across her shoulders, then turned to Lauren and did the same.

They were both silent as they came out of the restaurant, and once away from the door, Lauren said brokenly, "Beth, I'm so sorry! I only have a credit card – Gerald won't let me have any cash! I'll get it back to you – I promise, I'll get Gerald to make out a cheque and send it to you!"

"Forget it," said Beth, "Honestly, it's okay. It's about time I paid anyway – you always pay!"

"But this was our Christmas celebration! I wanted to treat you – I never imagined in my wildest dreams that they wouldn't be able to take my card! We should have waited –

they'd phone the bank and get clearance then my card would have been accepted. We should have waited!" Lauren was visibly distressed until Beth took her arm and hugged it to her side as she said in a soothing voice, "Don't worry about it, we need to get going to get these gifts or we'll run out of time. Just forget it, don't let something like that spoil our day!"

"I'll get Gerald to send a cheque – I promise! There's no way I'm allowing you to be out of pocket for today. I keep telling him I need to have cash, but he won't allow it! Everything has to be done by card – I can have anything I want on a card, but I can't do something like put a pound in the Salvation Army collection tin! Mad, isn't it?"

"Why is he so against cash?" asked Beth, "I know they say we live in a plastic world – but we're not a cashless society yet!"

"He says there's less chance of being mugged if you don't have actual cash………I don't know, he just insists on having receipts!" Lauren said miserably.

"Hmm, that's a bit of a poor excuse – I mean a mugger doesn't ask if you're carrying cash before mugging you – it's a spontaneous random act, not a pre-planned crime!" Beth shook her head sceptically.

They arrived at the toy shop and were approached almost immediately by a sales assistant asking if she could be of assistance. Beth told her the toys that they were interested in and the young lady went off to bring a selection of the American fashion dolls first. Lauren tried her best to show an interest in the toys, but she was dwelling on what had happened in the restaurant. *I can't let this happen again,* she thought, *I'm going to have to insist that Gerald gives me an allowance in cash! I'll have it out with him tonight!* She felt better having made this decision, so she forced her attention on to the fairy castles that the sales assistant had brought out next.

Once both toys had been selected, Lauren asked the assistant to gift wrap them which she smilingly agreed to. When she came back, the toys were fabulously parcelled up in sparkling Christmas paper with glistening bows and a beautiful gift card attached to each one ready for Lauren to write her Christmas message. Lauren handed her card for payment and took in a deep breath hoping that the 'connection' that the restaurant had problems with wasn't affecting the whole of the Metro Centre, but all was fine and the sales assistant handed her back her card and receipt with a very grateful smile.

Beth looked at her watch. "It's nearly half past two – do you need anything else, or shall we have a slow walk back to the bus stand?"

"We can go for the bus," said Lauren, "And I WILL get Gerald to send you a cheque – did you pick up the bill, by the way, I'll need it to prove we spent the money!"

"Good grief! Will he not just take your word?" asked Beth incredulously as she delved into her handbag and brought out a crumpled piece of paper which she shoved at Lauren.

"Well, it's just easier if I can show him ………he's not tight with money, he just has a thing about receipts for everything!"

Beth shook her head slowly. "That's so weird to me because in our house it's me that controls the finances – we have a joint account for all the household bills and food and such, but I handle it all. Talking of which – I'll have to call at a cash machine – the restaurant bill cleaned me out and I always need cash for the girls' clubs and activities!"

"Oh, Beth, I'm so sorry!" Lauren's shoulders slumped again, but Beth nudged her and said, "Enough! Let's just forget it, we're both fit and healthy, that's far more important than money!"

After stopping at a cash machine for Beth to withdraw some more cash, they made their way to the bus terminal and chatted idly until it was time for Beth to board. They hugged and Beth thanked her for the girls' presents and wished her a safe journey to Italy and Lauren in turn wished her sister a very happy Christmas and said she hoped the girls would enjoy the gifts. She stayed and waved to Beth as the bus departed, then made her way to the car park for her car deep in thought about the best way to approach the money issue with Gerald.

When he told her to leave work the week before they were married, she had no income going into her account each month so it wasn't very long before her account was dry. She asked him if he would give her an allowance for spending and he laughed and said, "You're my wife, not my daughter! You don't need an allowance – you have a card, buy whatever you want! As long as you bring the receipt home I don't mind what you spend!"

She had imagined that was how moneyed people lived – everything by card, except one lunch date she was having with some of Gerald's client's wives and she noticed that Louise Downey always paid her share of the bill in cash while all the others used their cards. When they were in the Ladies room Lauren had brought up the subject of cash, saying she never had any to be able to leave a tip for the rest-room attendant and Louise told her she had insisted that her husband had a cash allowance transferred into her bank each month to give her the option of using cash or card. "I love to use a big purse where the notes stand up – I hate folded money - and a section for my cards. I don't bother with small change – it's grubby and heavy so I stick that in charity boxes!"

She had related this tale to Gerald when she got home and asked if she could have an allowance paid into her bank, and Gerald had become angry and said he had already had this discussion with her and he didn't want to discuss it again. They'd only been married for nine months then and it was the first time she'd seen him angry and she was taken aback at how quickly his temper was roused.

She had reached her car by this time and she suddenly remembered about Jon. Once she was inside the car, she sent a text message asking if he was free for a call. Within moments, her phone rang and the screen displayed '*Jan calling*'. With a lurch of her heart she answered the call.

"Hello, Jon?" she said timorously.

"Hi, Lauren, it's great to hear from you. I'm in my room at the University – no-one around and it's completely private. How are you?" Jon's voice sounded strangely familiar to her as though it came from someone she'd always known.

She intended to say that she was fine, that everything was okay, but her voice would have given her away. "I'm sitting in my car at the Metro Centre at Gateshead. I've had lunch with my sister – we met here so I could buy my nieces their Christmas presents."

"That's nice," said Jon and she could tell he was smiling. "Was it a nice lunch?"

"It was supposed to be our Christmas celebration – I wanted to treat her to a special lunch, so we went to a pricey restaurant and ordered a three course lunch……….." She hesitated, wondering whether she should open up pandora's box – but before she could help herself the words came tumbling out and she told him about the card machine being out of order, Gerald's refusal to give her cash, his obsession with receipts, his temper when she tried to raise an issue with him………….one after the other of all the grievances that she'd held in for so long, till she finally flopped back in her seat exhausted by her outburst.

"I see," said Jon, "I don't wonder that you're not very happy – that's a lot of resentment to be carrying around!"

"The thing is," she continued, "I just got on with it – I thought that was how people in that kind of circle lived, I thought I would get used to it eventually, but then when Kate died……………." She tapered off, unable to continue.

"Yeah," he said slowly, "Losing someone you love changes everything, doesn't it?"

"Jon, do you ever get the feeling that you want to run – keep on running till you'd left it all behind you?" she asked.

There was a small laugh. "Goodness me! I do indeed! Especially after Sadie died – I'd already had the shock of finding out about Sue's crime and her subsequent imprisonment, but losing Sadie…………….Did you ever see the film *Forrest Gump*?" he asked suddenly.

"Yes, Kate and I watched it one night and we were shouting "Run, Forrest, run!" - joining in with the crowds, sitting on the edge of our sofa, tears streaming down our faces!" Lauren gave a small laugh at the memory. "Yes, it's just like that, isn't it………just wanting to run and run and run, till the problems are so far in the past that they don't exist any more!"

There was a few moments silence then Jon said softly, "What are you going to do?"

Lauren chewed on her bottom lip, knowing what she ought to do, but wondering if she was courageous enough to actually do anything at all. She took a deep breath in.

"I'm going to try and talk to him tonight – after dinner. I'm going to tell him that I'm not happy with the way things are…………see if he'll make a monthly allowance for me – just so that I've got some independence and choices! See – I have no choices!"

"Well, just be careful – if he's prone to losing his temper, don't put yourself at risk!" said Jon sounding rather concerned.

"Oh, he's never hit me – he's not violent!" she said sounding defensive.

"All the same, take care. Will you ring me again, to let me know you're okay?" he asked.

Yes, I will – I can't ring you on an evening when he's at home, but if you're available during the day…….."

"I'm usually free between two and four p.m. most days, unless I've got tutorials, but if so you'll get my answer-machine that you can leave a message telling me when I can ring you back."

"Alright, I'll try and ring you tomorrow – let you know how it went. I'd better go now, it'll start to come in dark pretty soon."

"Okay, take care, drive safely. I'll talk to you tomorrow, hopefully."

They ended the call and Lauren hugged her phone to her chest, smiling wistfully. If only Gerald was like that…………but that was asking WAY too much!

Later that evening Lauren cleared the dining table while Gerald went into his office to do some paperwork. Over dinner she had told him about the restaurant and how she was left feeling embarrassed when her sister had to pay the bill, and he had looked at her in bewilderment and asked why didn't she just wait till they contacted the bank, it was a simple procedure. She'd told him that Beth had to be home for the girls so they didn't have time to wait but added that she had the bill to show him if he could just write a cheque out to repay her sister. Gerald had tutted in annoyance and muttered something, but she chose to ignore the jibe and carried on with her meal.

Once the kitchen was cleaned and tidy she went to his office and hesitantly tapped on the door before pushing it open. He looked up in alarm and used his knee to push the lower desk drawer closed as he snapped, "What do you want?"

She held out the restaurant bill and said, "Can you make the cheque out for Beth then I can get it in the post tomorrow, please?"

He sighed heavily and slid the top drawer open and took out a cheque book. He looked at the bill and wrote the amount as he said curtly, "Who shall I make it payable to?" and she replied, "Bethany Dunston." He handed the cheque to her without another word, so she thanked him and then said, "Will you be long? I thought we could watch some TV together – there's film on in half an hour."

Gerald looked at her for a few seconds, then a flicker of a smile crossed his face and he said, "Okay, sweetie, just give me a while to finish up here. Get a nice bottle of wine open for us."

Lauren felt a surge of relief as she recognised his mood had changed and he would probably be cheery and good-humoured and she could relax. She walked over to the bureau on the far wall and took out an envelope and a sheet of writing paper. The desk drawers were always kept locked but the bureau was available for her to use if she needed stationery. It was quite a formidable room, very obviously Gerald's domain with no curios or trinkets, everything was practical and business-like – a large dark oak desk devoid of anything except the opened desk diary and an angle-poise lamp, set in front of the French windows and behind the desk stood a high-backed padded office chair. The huge button-back sofa took up most of one wall with a fleecy throw draped over the back that Gerald used when he drank too much and slept in the office, and a matching wing-backed chair stood next to the bureau on the other wall.

When they were first married she had pointed out some souvenirs and curiosities when they were on honeymoon saying they would look sweet in his office and he had laughed and said his office was a place of work and unfitting for junk like that. She was disappointed but accepted that his office was his man-cave and didn't suggest anything like that again. He was already living in the house when they got married but he allowed her freedom to revamp the bedroom and lounge to her taste, however, the rest of the house – including the kitchen – she had to leave as it was. She hadn't made many changes – she had to admit that she couldn't improve much, it was a fabulous house, but she changed the colour of the drapes and the soft furnishings to try to put a bit of her own stamp on things.

When he came out of his office a while later, Lauren had set out an array of nibbles and opened and poured the wine so when Gerald came in he smiled and said, "Ah, a cosy night snuggling on the sofa! Just what I need." He settled himself on the sofa so she could nestle into him just as the film started. Lauren sighed in contentment. *This is what it should be like all the time*, she thought, *then I wouldn't ever want to leave him.* Perhaps it would be, perhaps his temper and his impatience were just part of settling into marriage and he would gradually be more understanding concerning her feelings of loss about Kate and her feelings of desertion from her parents. They would start to do things like walk along the beach together, or the promenade………..as she tried to visualise this happening, her thoughts conjured up the image of Jon and her walking towards the café as they had done on Sunday. This caused her to think about Jon's swarthy dark looks and how gentle he seemed……….how he had loved Sadie………..and she became conscious of a feeling of envy. She wanted to be loved like that! But hadn't Gerald loved her like that when they were first together? Why did she feel that he didn't love her like that now? When did it change?

She heard a strange gurgling noise and when she looked over her shoulder, Gerald had fallen asleep . His head had lolled back against the cushion and his mouth hung open and drools of spittle had accumulated in the corner of his lips and he was making a choking sound. Lauren tutted in disgust and nudged him. His eyes shot open and he lifted his head.

"Whaaa?" he blustered, "What's wrong?"

"You fell asleep. You were snoring!" she said, "Aren't you watching the film?"

"Yes, I just nodded off for a minute – I work hard, you know!" He leaned forward and picked up his wine glass and Lauren, sensing that he could easily slip into a bad mood because of her criticism, kissed him on the neck as he settled back into the cushions and said, "I know you do. And I'm very proud of what you do." This did the trick and she saw his ego being smoothed as he nodded in agreement with her. She handed him the little tray of nibbles and took some herself as they resumed watching the film.

An hour or so later when the film was finished and she sensed that Gerald was in the best mood he could be in, she decided to broach the subject of him giving her a cash allowance.

"What on earth do you want a cash allowance for?" he asked as he popped a handful of peanuts into his mouth.

"Well, for things like…….putting money in charity boxes…….or to give to the attendants in the ladies cloakrooms………or being able to park in places that have cash meters instead of always using the big car parks………." Her voice dwindled as she realised that she was giving pathetic and weak reasons.

Gerald's face registered incredulity and her heart sank before he had uttered a word. "Putting money in charity boxes?" he exclaimed disbelievingly, "Do you think I slave all day to put money in charity boxes? You have a credit card for anything that you could possibly want to buy, yet you want me to trail down to the bank and withdraw cash just so that you can put it in charity boxes?" His voice was starting to rise and she knew she had no chance of furthering the argument unless she wanted to bear the brunt of his fury and she knew she would end up in tears if she did.

"It doesn't matter," she mumbled, getting up off the sofa.

"No!" he said loudly, "I want to know why this sudden urge to have cash - what is it you're doing that you don't want me to know about?"

She turned to face him with her eyes wide in surprise. "What am I doing? What do you mean – I'm not doing anything! How could I? You know everything I do!" She felt her face growing warm.

"Err……..excuse me……but have you forgotten that little trip to the coast on Sunday that I knew nothing about………..and the lies you told to cover it up? Have you forgotten that? Because I haven't!" He was shouting now and stood up to face her. "I don't know what you think you're playing at, but you'd better sort yourself out because I won't put up with any deceit – you'll be out of this door before you can blink!"

"I'm not doing anything!" she shouted, "It's not fair – you're always accusing me of doing things and I'm not doing anything!"

"Well, that's the truth – you're not doing *anything!* I'M the one who works here, I'M the one who earns the money, all you do is spend it! And you're never satisfied with that – now you tell me you want me to give you cash so that you can give MY money away to beggars and charities!"

"Gerald…….why are you so cruel to me?" she said brokenly, "I only want………" She had started to crumble and hated herself for crying so easily.

"I know what you want – you want a good kick up the backside!" His face was distorted with anger as he took a step towards her and she backed away from him.

"No! Please don't…….. If you hurt me…….I'll …….I'll leave you…….I'll divorce you!" she whimpered.

"You'll divorce me?" He laughed cynically. "Go on then…….divorce me……..you'll walk away penniless. Oh, but isn't that how you came into the marriage – penniless?" He pushed his face up to hers and she cowered away from him.

"We're married – I've got rights………I'm entitled to…….." His harsh laugh silenced her.

"You're entitled to…….what? Half of everything?" he sneered, "Well, guess what – that's half of nothing!"

"What do you mean – there's the house…….the cars…….." she began.

"Yep! All belonging to my father! He owns everything! This is HIS house, he just lets us live here. And the cars belong to the business! There's NOTHING in my name! NOTHING!" He stood with his arms akimbo with a smug, gloating expression on his face. "This is what father was protecting me from! Thank God I listened to him! So, go on! Do it! ………….leave me! Go on! Go back to the drab existence you had before I plucked you out of your misery and gave you the life of a successful business man's wife, where you're pampered and coddled and all you have to do is spend money!"

Lauren shook her head in disbelief at what she was hearing – his father owned everything? She had assumed the house was his – theirs, it never entered her head that it could be his father's property. Gerald had kept all this a secret!

Not really, her inner voice said, *you never discussed finances, you were just happy to go along with everything and live the life he trained you for!* She turned away from him and slowly sank into the armchair with her head in her hands. She heard him go out of the room then she flinched nervously as she heard his office door slam shut. She stared unseeingly at the rug in front of the marble fireplace, her mind whirling. She felt as if she was on shifting sands………what was she going to do?

She could leave him and go…………where? She'd have to get a job and find a flat somewhere……..how could she get a flat with no money for rent? Her mind was racing. She'd have to get a job first……she'd have to get a job while she lived here and save up for a deposit and the first month's rent. She'd have to do that without Gerald knowing about it otherwise he'd stop her. She'd have to act as though she was happy being married to him and continue to run the house and carry on her normal, married life with Gerald and somehow fit in going to work secretly! Then when she had enough money she could leave.

Or ……….she could just ………..stay! Carry on as before, being pampered and coddled…………. and humiliated and verbally abused and demeaned, because that was the price for a comfortable lifestyle with Gerald. The choice was hers.

Her heart was heavy as she turned off all the lights and slowly went up the stairs. At the top of the staircase she looked down at the large entrance hall and the etched glass doors leading to the porch, the spindle-legged half-moon table against the wall with the huge spray of silk flowers and the shallow glass bowl that held the car-keys and mail so Gerald could pick it up as he came in. This hall was the size of the living-room she could expect in a rented flat........could she go back to that?

She glanced at the office door which was closed but the light shone from underneath the door so she knew Gerald was in there. He'd be drinking again and he would probably fall asleep on the sofa in there. Good! She didn't want to see him or hear him taunt her again tonight, not with the amount of hatred that was rushing through her veins just now! She reached the bedroom and with a choking sob she threw herself down on the bed. She looked across at the bedside clock.......ten twenty-five. It was too late to ring Jon, he would probably be in bed. The same with her sister – she'd be in bed. That was it – only two people she could ring for advice or even a chat when her life was falling apart..........all those she lunched with or went to beauty parlours with.........they weren't friends, she always had to act a part when she was with them.

Kate was right! Kate knew what he would be like. Yet she had never bad-mouthed him, she'd never tried to tell Lauren how to live her life, she'd accepted the choices Lauren had made and would have been there to support her – if she hadn't died! She felt the piercing knife-pain in her heart and her face crumpled. *"Why did you have to die? Why did you have to leave me?"* she sobbed, *"Kate – I need you! I need you to tell me what to do!"*

She went into the bathroom and filled the bath, hoping that a hot bath would help to relax her and take away some of the tension in her body. As she leaned across to get the bottle of bath oil from the shelf, she heard a 'plop' and gasped in horror as she saw her phone that had been on the side of the bath now lying at the bottom of the bath. She hastily plunged her arm in to retrieve it as tears rushed to her eyes and she sobbed as she wrapped it in a towel and hugged it to her chest saying over and over, "No, no, no! Not my phone!"

With a wail she ran downstairs crying, "Gerald! Gerald!" and as he came to his office door she cried, "My phone! My phone fell in the bath!"

"For God's sake, Lauren! You're so stupid! Well, there's no chance of fixing that! "

"There must be something………" she babbled looking around wildly, "Can't you do something?"

"What do you think I am? A miracle-worker? No! There's nothing anyone can do when you plunge a phone into the bath! You'll need a new one!"

"But my numbers……..what about my numbers?" She looked at him beseechingly, but he snorted and turned on his heel.

"They're all gone, Lauren, everything's gone! If you're stupid enough……….. oh, just go to bed before you cost me any more money!"

She sobbingly made her way back up the stairs her heart breaking. She'd lost contact with Jon – she had destroyed his card when she stored the number on her phone and now that was gone. And her sister – she couldn't recall her number, there were eleven digits in a mobile phone number, she couldn't recall them – or anyone's! She was completely isolated now. She staggered into her bedroom and threw herself on the bed and wept until sheer exhaustion took over and she fell into a fitful sleep.

The following week was an enormous mental and emotional strain for Lauren. Every evening when Gerald came in from work she asked him if he'd bought her a new phone, and the answer was always the same – he'd been too busy but would do it the following day. She knew he was punishing her by making her wait. Her life continued as before because of the large desk diary – she knew what appointments she had, she could still go to the hairdresser or the beauty parlour or go shopping! None of that changed because she didn't have a phone, she just couldn't contact anyone. The house phone was there – the landline – so she wasn't without a telephone, but her mobile phone had held all her contacts.

Gerald was acting as if the disclosure that his father owned everything made no difference to their lives, but for Lauren it changed everything. She'd been raised to be independent – her father had taught both his daughters to stand on their own feet from their teenage years and when she'd married Gerald they were happy that she was marrying a successful businessman, but she'd held back from them the financial control that Gerald wielded over her. She could imagine the horror on their faces if she were to tell them that Gerald wasn't the successful businessman they all thought he was who owned a big house, but he was in fact an employee in an accommodation-provided job with no security unless he did everything his father told him to do and waited until he'd died to get the inheritance! She was already struggling with Gerald's suppression, but to know that he himself was totally dominated by his father doubled her feelings of subjugation.

They were due to fly to Italy in ten days – she didn't want to go on this trip – it was a combined business trip and holiday. Now she knew it would be funded by the business and everything would be on Gerald's expenses account she didn't want any part of it, it somehow felt tainted. She'd been thinking of feigning illness at the last moment so that he would flounce off in a mood but she didn't know if she could carry it off – she would have to look ill when she normally had a healthy colour and appearance.

She had nothing in the diary on the Thursday so decided to give the bedrooms a thorough cleaning. She was on her hands and knees going around the skirtings with a damp cloth and had pulled the bedside cabinets away from the wall. She couldn't move the bed as it was a solid oak frame so she'd lain on the floor and crawled under the bed to reach the skirting board at the back. As she wriggled back out from under the bed she felt a crick in her neck, so she'd flipped over on to her back to make it easier on her neck when she noticed that Gerald's bedside cabinet drawer was slightly open and the underside showed a piece of coloured tape. She pulled the drawer out a bit more and noticed there was a bump in the middle as if something had been taped under the drawer.

She picked at the edge of the tape and as it came away it revealed a key and as she turned it over in her fingers she wondered if this might be Gerald's office desk key. She quickly shimmied out and scrambled to her feet and ran down the stairs and into Gerald's office. This must be the spare key as he carried all his keys together on one large bunch. With a fast beating heart she approached the desk and inserted the key into the lock. The key turned.

She ignored the top two drawers – it was the bottom drawer that Gerald had suspiciously nudged shut with his knee the day she came in to ask him to make the cheque out for Beth. She pulled the bottom drawer open slowly. Inside there was a book and two bottles of what looked to be very expensive wine in boxes and at the back was a large cardboard box, roughly the size of a shoebox. She took it out very carefully and placed it on the desk and with shaking hands she opened it. She gasped as she saw that inside it was crammed with bundles of banknotes, all standing on edge. She took out a bundle of twenty-pound notes held together with an elastic band and counted them – five hundred pounds! As her eyes travelled over the rest, she counted what was there – twenty seven bundles, plus loose notes lying at the side. That was a total of thirteen thousand five hundred pounds, plus the rest…………where had this come from? Why did Gerald have so much cash at home when he wouldn't allow her to have any cash at all?

She took out the book that was lying next to the wine and opened it at random. It was an A5 notebook with various date entries next to names and numbers that Lauren couldn't understand but as she flipped through the pages she began to recognise some of the names as clients who did business with Gerald. The last entry was dated the previous day with names and numbers that meant nothing to her at first, then a slow realisation crept over her – this looked like Gerald was 'fiddling the books'! He was either selling wine on the side for cash deals or he was taking backhanders……. it didn't matter how he got it, the point was that it was dishonest! He was stealing from his father!

She flopped down into the big wing-backed chair in front of the desk and as her heart bumped and jolted painfully she imagined what would happen if Gerald's father found out that his second son was also thieving from the business – he'd had no hesitation in disinheriting his first-born son and had refused to set eyes on him since. He would do the same with Gerald – and she would be turfed out with him! Where would they go? What would they do? She could feel the panic start to rise inside her and she hastily stood up then began to pace the floor. Her life with Gerald was becoming barely tolerable even with the glitz and the wealthy trappings that came with it, but a life of poverty and homelessness with him? Unthinkable!

All of a sudden she had a flash of hope and excitement. This was her chance……………she could take this money and leave! Leave Gerald! She doubted that he would report it to the police as a theft as he wasn't supposed to have it in the first place! It was perfect! She looked at her watch – quarter to eleven. She could do it, she had enough time to pack and get out before Gerald came home. It had to be today - she was scared to face him with this knowledge in case she gave anything away. But where would she go? She could go to her sister's just for tonight and tell her everything, then she'd book into a hotel nearby till she'd made plans. Yes! Yes!

She could rent a flat with this money – she could get a job! She could buy a new phone and ring York University and ask for Dr Jonathan Gibson to call her on this number! She could get back in touch with Jon! She could have a new life! Perhaps when Jon sorted out his life with his wife – just maybe they could get together! Lauren could feel the excitement bubble up inside her as she realised that this was the answer to her prayers. She wouldn't EVER have to see Gerald again!

Energy and enthusiasm flooded her veins and she left the box on the desk and ran up the stairs laughing joyfully. She grabbed a suitcase then paused ………..she'd better not take the car – if that belonged to the business she could be accused of stealing. She'd take a taxi to the station and go by train! She could do that – she had cash! With that decision made she began to rifle through her wardrobe. She pushed aside all the glamorous evening gowns and cocktail dresses – she didn't want any of them taking up valuable suitcase space! She placed a smart trouser suit on the bed for her to change into when she was packed and showered, then when the suitcase was filled, she selected a smaller case and filled that with toiletries and underwear. As she packed she realised that she didn't have what some people would term as memorabilia – nothing of any emotional value. *Just like my life here with Gerald!* she thought.

Lastly, she got an Aspinal designer leather tote bag – this had been her last birthday present from Gerald when he'd had a business trip in London. This would be large enough to carry her huge make-up bag, passport..........and the money. She ran down the stairs with the empty tote bag, then rushed into the office. She hastily grabbed all the wads of notes and stuffed them into the bag. She then placed the empty box back in the drawer, closed it and locked it. She paused with her hand on the drawer – Gerald would be furious when he realised she'd taken this money and he might try to find her to get the money back!

The book! If she took the notebook with all the incriminating evidence in, she had proof of his theft from the business! If he DID track her down, she could threaten to send this evidence to his father! That would silence him – that was her insurance! She pulled the drawer open again and picked up the book, shoving it to the bottom of her tote bag, then closed and locked the drawer. She looked around the room to ensure that everything looked normal and with a smug grin, she closed the door behind her.

Running back up the stairs she took the small key and pushed it back into the tape and resealed it under the drawer, lying on the floor to look up at it to make sure it was in the correct place. Perfect! It looked untouched. She placed a small hand towel over the bundles of money in the bottom of the tote bag, leaving the loose notes on top for easy access, then put in her passport, make-up bag and hairbrush. Her heart was still beating madly and she sat down on the bed, willing herself to calm down.

Once she was showered and changed, she took the largest case down the stairs and came back up for the smaller one and the tote bag. She looked around the bedroom, making sure that everything looked normal, and with a grin she closed the bedroom door and shouldering the tote bag she walked calmly down the stairs. She went back into the office where the house telephone was and rang for a taxi from the list of numbers that were on the card next to the phone. The operator said the taxi would be with her within fifteen minutes and asked if this was on account. She hastily said it wasn't – this would be cash. She didn't want the address of where she was going to show on the taxi account when it came in.

Her final job was to take a piece of writing paper from the bureau and to pen a letter to Gerald. She was only doing this because she didn't want Gerald to report her as missing – if he would even do that! But also, she wanted him to know that this was a calm decision she had taken and not the result of an emotional response after he had bullied her. She made several attempts, firstly detailing all the grievances she had held for so long, but finally decided that he wasn't even worthy of long explanations – that would be detailed in the divorce papers! So she stuffed all the crumpled papers that she had rejected into her bag and simply wrote:

Gerald

I have left you and our marriage. I can't take any more of your insufferable behaviour. Please don't ty to find me – you will hear in due course from my solicitor regarding a divorce.

Lauren.

She left this note on the spindle-legged hall table, so he would see it when he came in, then took her luggage outside and placed it on the drive. She closed the front door and as she turned to face the drive and the garden, the sun suddenly broke through the clouds and beamed down then just as suddenly the clouds covered it up and it was gone! But the message was clear – Lauren's heart filled with joy and she breathed deeply turning her face towards the skies.

"I did it, Kate – I heard you, and I did it!" she said. She turned back to the door and pushed the key through the letter-box. That was it! The end of the marriage! All done!

Just then the taxi pulled up and the driver got out to place her luggage in the boot, smiling at her and asking if she was off anywhere nice. She told him she was joining her parents in the Canaries – making it up as she went along, but it didn't matter, it was idle chatter. He dropped her at the local railway station which was only a five-minute drive away and she handed him a twenty-pound note from her bag. He held out a ten-pound note and rummaged for coin change, but she said, "It's ok, keep it all!" He thanked her profusely for such a large tip and she smiled at him, enjoying the feeling of independence that such an act gave her.

Turning to the station entrance, she clicked the handle of her suitcase in place and picked up the smaller one. This small, local train station was the first step in her new life. She took a deep breath and looked up again at the sky and the weak winter sun came out from behind the dark clouds again, almost as if the sky was validating the decision she had made, confirming it was the right one.

"Thank you, Kate," she whispered, "I knew you'd never let me down."

*****

The Numbers Game

Eva woke up with a start. It was still dark in the bedroom and she felt the familiar fingers of dread creeping up from her stomach into the back of her head. She didn't know what time it was and she was scared to look at the clock because it might display numbers that she didn't want to see. She closed her eyes again and turned away from where the clock stood on her bedside cabinet. She wanted to look at the clock to see if it was happening again, but if she did and it was, she would panic! It was more significant today than any other day. She could feel her heart hammering against her ribs as she tried to work out how she was going to face the day ahead.

She had dreaded this coming day since she had realised it was a palindromic date. The second of February 2020 – 02/02/2020. This date read the same forwards and backwards! It had to be significant because of the problems that repeating numbers on a digital clock brought to her! She had worried about how often this kind of date occurred so she had Googled it and found there are 29 palindromic dates in the 21st century in the dd/mm/yyyy format. It didn't specify what they were and she was too afraid to work it out because it would only serve to lay out a minefield in front of her so she worked on the premise that ignorance was the safest way. There were only 12 palindromic dates in the mm/dd/yyyy format and she had at one time even contemplated moving to the US or Canada where they used the latter just to reduce the number of times she would have to endure this torment!

It started several years ago when she would wake through the night – which she did most nights - and looking at her bedside clock she would see 3:33 or 4:44. It didn't seem significant at first but it kept happening, then she started waking at 2:22 , sometimes 1:11 until it seemed that every single time she woke up there would be repeating numbers on the clock. She used to chuckle when it happened at first and after work she would call in to see her friend, Fran, and tell her it had happened again. They had Googled it and were told that some spiritualists thought that people are seeing more repeating numbers nowadays because of a new spiritual awareness or 'awakening'. They believed it was because humans are evolving on a spiritual level now and the numbers are messages from a Higher Source.

Fran had been diagnosed with breast cancer over four years ago and when she was recovering from the chemotherapy treatment Eva had called in nearly every day to see her. They had been friends for over thirty-five years and had lived on the same street for the past twenty-five of them. They had supported each other through many life crises -

when Eva's husband was unfaithful and she divorced him, when Eva's son went though his rebellious phase, when Fran's daughter got pregnant at fifteen, then substantially more so when Fran was first diagnosed. They were as close as any two people could be and when Eva had these episodes when she constantly saw the repeating clock numbers they used to laugh and say Eva was 'receiving' messages but hadn't been given the power to interpret them.

It caused a great deal of merriment when Gill and Fiona also came to visit Fran and they would open a couple of bottles of wine and try to work out what these messages could be. Gill thought Eva was being told that a new love was on the horizon for her, but Eva said he needn't bother as she wasn't interested! Fiona thought it was 'from the other side' – perhaps one of her deceased parents trying to contact her! However, Fran thought it was simply co-incidence and nothing more and the only way that Eva could fix it was to get rid of the digital clock and buy a traditional clock-faced clock! But Eva had told her she needed a radio-alarm to wake her up and she'd never found one with an analogue clock – they all came with digital clocks on them. And it wasn't every night it happened – just sporadically, but when it did it happened over several nights in a row, then it would cease for weeks, sometimes months.

When Fran's illness suddenly turned out to be terminal cancer and she was given only months to live, Eva knew with a sickening certainty that this was the warning she had been given by the repeating numbers she had been seeing. Even during the day – every time she looked at a digital clock, no matter whether it was at work, in a shop window, on the television, every glance at a digital clock anywhere showed repeating numbers. Then once the doctors gave Fran the devastating prognosis, the repeating numbers ceased as if they had made their point. This proved to Eva that it was a prophecy!

From then it became an emotional roller-coaster, trying to keep Fran's spirits up but at the same time prepare her family for life without their mum. When it started again during the short time Fran had left and Eva saw repeating numbers every time she looked at any clock and it made her wail in anguish every time it happened, until she could no longer bear to look at the clock through the night, so she had no idea how long it carried on. Then one night she accidently caught sight of the clock as she missed her footing as she got out of bed and the clock showed 3:10, so she knew she was in a reprieve from the numbers game. But Fran was in a hospice by this time.

Fran's daughters were twenty-three and twenty-six at the time and it was the younger daughter who'd had the child at fifteen – a boy then 7 years old and Fran's pride and joy. The only time that Fran broke down was when she had said she would never see Connor as a young man and Eva held her as she wept wretchedly in her arms. Connor lived with his mum, Shelley, in a rented house three streets away and Shelley came every morning after taking Connor to school to spend some time with her mum and do chores for her.

Fran's other daughter, Paige, was a teacher at a primary school and was married to a policeman and they lived in Cheshire. Paige normally came to visit her mum every six or seven weeks when there was a school break and she had spoken to Eva about feeling guilty that she couldn't do more for her mum while she was ill, but Eva had told her she could only do what she could do. But inside Eva guessed that Paige would be racked with guilt afterwards and regret that she hadn't put her mum before her career while she could.

Suddenly, a loud burst of music made Eva jump and drag her back to the present and she realised that her alarm had gone off so it must be 6:00 therefore it was safe to look at the clock. Once it got past 5:55 she was safe until 10:10. She hadn't managed to go back to sleep but had drifted down memory lane and she felt the familiar tightness in her chest and the gripping ache in her throat whenever she re-lived the last few months of Fran's life. Because that's all she got –

three months, two weeks and a day from being told it was terminal till she died.

Eva dragged herself out of bed, her eyes still full with unshed tears and staggered into the bathroom. As she looked in the mirror, the face that looked back at her was etched in misery with dark circles under the eyes, an unhealthy pallor to the skin and wrinkles and lines that she was sure weren't there the week before. She ran her fingers through her hair and tried to give herself a mental shake to rid herself of this awful feeling of foreboding.

Staring into the mirror, she suddenly realised to her dismay that today was Sunday! She didn't have to go to work! She didn't need to get up at six o'clock! She could have woken up naturally without the alarm – it probably would have been at a similar time as she never stayed in bed late, but the point was she didn't need the alarm on a Sunday! She felt cheated, somehow, made worse by the fact that there was nobody to blame but herself!

Although the weather was quite mild for February – the sky was overcast but it was dry - Eva felt chilled to the bone even though the central heating was on. She went downstairs in her dressing-gown and padded round the kitchen not really interested in eating but telling herself she should have some breakfast. She made some toast and coffee then took it into the sitting-room and turned on the electric fire and curling herself up on the armchair she nibbled some of the toast and drank the coffee. She turned on the television, flicked through the channels but paid no heed to what came on the screen.

She walked over to the window and looked out at the still-dark street outside, partially expecting something to be different, but not really being surprised when everything looked exactly the same as it had the day before. She picked up some magazines that were lying on the coffee table and skimmed through them, then threw them down again. She tried to tell herself to go for a walk – but dismissed the idea before it had even become a coherent sentence inside her head.

She wanted to cry! She wanted to talk to someone but there was nobody who would listen to her – nobody who would understand the significance of a day like today! *Fran would have understood!* the voice inside her head said. Fran would also have told her to get a grip, but that would have been okay coming from Fran because Eva knew that Fran believed her fear - not what she was afraid of, but she understood the fear it generated.

I'm really mad at you, Fran, she said inside her head. *Three Christmases now without you and it's no easier! If* you'd been here you would have let me sit with you all day today – just to prove that there was nothing to be scared of!

She started to laugh at her own irrationality, but the laughing soon turned to weeping and she slowly sank down on the chair and gave in to the futility of everything – her grief over her best friend dying, her fear of the repeating numbers and what she was scared they might foretell and the paralysing effect it had on her mind. She kept remembering Fran's words – " There's nothing mystical or magical about it – it's just a number that denotes the time of day or night!" she used to say to Eva. But why does it keep happening? Why do I see these repeating numbers each time I look at the clock? her mind was screaming.

Every time she went through a period of waking to see repeating numbers on the alarm clock night after night, it seemed to be followed by some bad news – or something going wrong, or a drama or trauma of some kind, to the extent that it caused her significant distress when one of these cycles began and created a build-up of anxiety each time she faced these dreaded numbers. That's why she couldn't take a chance on finding a set of repeating numbers on the clock throughout last night – not with today having such a momentous date! It would surely herald doom!

The day passed slowly with Eva prowling from one room to the next, occasionally trying to lose herself in a television show but not being able to concentrate. She gave up at one-thirty in the afternoon and took herself off to bed. She felt exhausted as she'd not had much sleep the night before, but on top of that her anxiety level when she was in one of these cycles was so high that it was debilitating. She crawled into bed and lay staring at the ceiling trying to focus on deep breathing to relax herself enough to be able to fall asleep.

Since Fran was first diagnosed with breast cancer four and a half years ago Eva had experienced several of these 'repeating number cycles' and nearly every time she got news or experienced some major life event. One time was when she found her fourteen-year old son had been taking drugs and ended up in hospital – another time her sister's husband had died suddenly. A couple of times she'd had a run of waking at 3:33 for three nights in a row, then it stopped and nothing dramatic occurred, but for several days her mind was as taut as a violin string.

Last winter, Eva had a cough and chest infection that carried on for several weeks. The doctor finally sent her for a chest X-ray and she was told the results would be sent to her doctor and she would be notified of the result on her next appointment with him two weeks later. She was convinced that she had something sinister and she was terrified of seeing fateful numbers when she woke through the night so when she got out of bed she would keep her eyes closed till she'd reached her bedroom door, taking tiny cautious steps with her arms stretched out in front of her in the customary floundering stagger of a sleepwalker. This continued for eight nights in a row, then one night she was facing the clock when she woke up so had no choice but to see what was in front of her eyes and to her relief she saw 3:07 on the clock and the next night it was 2:55 so when she went for her doctor's appointment and was told her X-ray was clear, she was thankful but not unduly surprised because the numbers had stopped repeating.

Her mind started to drift back to the times before she saw repeating numbers when she'd had any life-changing traumas and from there she tried to work out when the problem had begun. As far as she could remember it happened just after she'd found Eddie had been having an affair. It was just before their fourteenth wedding anniversary – ten years ago and her life was shattered. Their daughter, Sofie, was twelve and their son, Mikey, was nearly nine and it was Sofie who seemed to be the worst affected by their breakup. She had loved her father and she felt his betrayal as deeply as Eva had – she had cried every night in bed for a month and had refused to see him. Mikey didn't seem to be bothered and appeared to adapt quite easily to his weekend visits to his dad's apartment, but after a few months his dad's girlfriend moved in and Mikey didn't get his dad's undivided attention any more and then Sofie decided to start visiting her dad which exacerbated the situation and Mikey became sullen and difficult and his behaviour became out of control.

By the time Mikey was fourteen and had been hospitalised through taking drugs he had been excluded from school on two occasions and had been referred to a Child Psychologist. Eva blamed Eddie for Mikey's behaviour but Eddie took no responsibility saying there were thousands of kids who came from broken homes and they weren't affected and he laid the blame at Eva's door saying she'd had the major caring role therefore it was her parenting that was at fault – she hadn't been consistent in her discipline. Eva was devastated and asked Mikey if he'd rather live with his father where perhaps he'd have more consistency with discipline from his father but Mikey flatly refused, so Eva told him he would have to change his ways or it might become the only solution.

This seemed to work and Mikey managed to pull himself together in the next couple of years and successfully finished his schooling and when he was seventeen he applied to join the Royal Navy. He completed his pre-assessments and basic training – which was at first a nerve and gut wrenching time for Eva as it was the first time he'd been away by himself and Plymouth was a long way from home, but he flourished under the intensive training and from there he chose to go into engineering in the Royal Navy. He kept in touch with his mother so Eva knew he was safe and he was enjoying the mix of college and shipboard learning, but she could feel a gulf widening between them as his independence grew. She was saddened by this but was intensely proud of the man he was becoming and reckoned this was the sacrifice she had to make as a mother.

Sofie had always been what a friend of Eva's had once described as 'biddable' – quiet and compliant with a generous nature. She cried a lot when her father first left, refusing to see him at all until one day she told Eva she wanted to visit him with Mikey. She did this for a few times but then when his girlfriend moved in she told her father she was allowing him to move on with his new life and she would keep in touch by phone only. Mandy, his girlfriend was relieved, as she was only twenty five and had no idea how to relate to a young teenager and Eva thought that Sofie had picked up on this but being so generous in nature she decided it would be easier all round if she withdrew.

She excelled at school and after A levels she went to University to study veterinary medicine. At present she was on placement with a Veterinary Practice in Nottingham and next year was her final year of the five-year course required but she had already told Eva that she would probably not be returning home to live as she was moving in with her boyfriend whom she had met in her first year at University. Eva was naturally upset at first but again took comfort in the fact that both of her children had carved successful lives for themselves – in spite of their father letting them down.

She was deeply saddened by the fact that she couldn't share her pride at her children's successes with Fran, because it had been Fran she had turned to every time something went wrong and Fran had been her pillar of support, even when she was suffering cancer. By the time Mickey had turned his life around and became the kind of son that Eva had prayed for, Fran had died and Eva couldn't share the good times with her.

Eva gradually brought herself back to the present. She'd not been able to drift off to sleep like she'd wanted to do and it was already starting to turn dark outside so she guessed it was somewhere around four o'clock in the afternoon. She daren't look at the clock on her bedside cabinet because it was a twenty-four hour clock and the bigger repeating number seemed more menacing, plus they went on for longer – up to 23:23! Suddenly she had a surge of defiance and before she could change her mind she quickly turned her head and saw 16:04 on the clock.

She sat up quickly and a slow grin spread over her face. The day had not produced any traumas or world-ending events for her and this had been confirmed by not giving her the urge to look at the clock when it was showing a repeating number. She threw the duvet back and swung her legs over the side of the bed. Thinking about her life as she had over the past couple of hours and the things that had gone well – in spite of the set-backs - had given her a burst of confidence. The fear she'd developed about the repeating numbers over the last four or five years she knew were tied up with anxiety and grief over her friend dying – her head knew all this but her emotions very often over-ruled her head and she couldn't think rationally.

"Right!" she said out loud, "We're going to start again!" She glared at the clock, the red numbers staring back defiantly at her and the little pulsing dots in the middle separating the hours from the minutes like blinks of innocence. "You don't scare me any more!" she told the clock and blew it a raspberry!

The next morning she boarded the bus to take her to work and found there were no seats available. It was a forty-five minute journey and not many people got off before the city so she didn't have much chance of a seat becoming vacant.

She took a deep breath in and moved down the aisle in the bus to try to find a more suitable spot for balancing herself from the swaying and lurching that would undoubtedly occur on the journey. As the bus set off, it caused her to stagger as she hadn't quite settled herself and she tried to grab an upright pole with her left hand which unfortunately was also carrying her large handbag. The handbag therefore smacked into the face and head of a man sitting in the seat below reading his newspaper.

"Oh, my goodness! I'm so sorry!" she gasped, "It was an accident! I'm so sorry! Are you hurt?" She managed to right herself and still hanging on to the pole, her handbag swinging dangerously, she leaned over and looked at his face. The man rubbed his cheek and eyebrow and smiled ruefully at her, gesturing to her handbag swinging violently back and forth with every movement of the bus.

"I think you'd better sit down! It might be safer if you do!" He smiled at her as he stood up and squeezed himself into the aisle arching his back so she could wriggle into the small space and lower herself in the seat, all the while saying she was sorry and he didn't have to give her his seat, but he continued to smile and concentrate on folding up his newspaper.

"You're very kind," she said looking up at him, a tiny glow of pleasure at his old-fashioned manners.

"You're very welcome," he said. After a few seconds he said, "Are you going to work?"

"Yes," she replied, "Are you?"

"No, I've an appointment – actually it's a job interview, I'm ready for a change and this came up at the right time."

"Well, you should get it – good deeds are always repaid!" she said to him with a confident nod of her head.

He gave a little chuckle and said, "Thank you, I'll hold on to that thought. Although it wasn't a good deed - it was a strategy to prevent my head from being battered by your handbag!" They both laughed at this and Eva grimaced.

"I'm so sorry about that, I don't usually use it as a weapon."

They chatted amicably all the way to the end of their journey and as they got off the bus, he turned to her and asked which way she was going. She said she was going to a small coffee-shop first as she was too early for work and the doors wouldn't be open yet, but if she got a later bus it could make her late if there were any traffic hold-ups.

"That's great, I'm early for my interview, so may I join you?" he asked and Eva felt herself flush.

"Yeah, that's fine, it's only a small place, but I know the owner and he's a lovely man and makes great coffee." She gestured over her shoulder, "It's down this way."

They set off, still chatting easily about her job as an estate agent and his current job as a buyer and the prospective job as a procurement officer and the difference between both jobs. He explained that he didn't normally travel by bus but thought it would be easier today when he wouldn't have to find somewhere to park his car. Eva told him it was the same for her – she left her car at home as there was nowhere to park near the office and they had a firm's car for viewing properties that they all shared. It meant they had to keep good records of viewings and out-of-office business so that they didn't double book the car. The staff all thought it was a strategy for not paying travel expenses that could so easily be fiddled! By the time they'd covered all this, they were at the coffee shop and had secured a small table by the window.

Eva had waved to Mario when she first entered and Mario waited till they were seated and came over to their table smiling widely at them.

"Ah, my morning is complete now the beautiful Eva has arrived," he beamed, "Would you like your usual?" As Eva nodded, he turned to her companion. "And you, sir, you would like the same?" Receiving an affirmative response, Mario flicked his tea-towel over his shoulder and went back behind the counter to make the coffees.

"By the way, I'm Eva, Eva Grainger," she said holding her hand out coyly.

"Hello, Eva, I'm David Westbrook," he said shaking her hand with a smile on his face and his eyes twinkling. "Do you come here often?" he added with a droll grin and a waggle of his head.

Eva gave a laugh. "Every morning, actually," she said. "I need my fortification before the day begins!"

"Aha! So I know where to find you," he said with an obvious fake accent and a twirl of a pretend moustache, causing Eva to giggle.

When Mario brought the coffees to them, David handed him a ten pound note and with a glance at Eva said, "Allow me, Eva."

"Thank you," she murmured enjoying the feeling of being indulged – it wasn't something that happened very often.

"Did you have a nice weekend?" asked David. "Did you know, by the way, that yesterday was a palindrome day?"

Eva nearly choked on her coffee and as she hastily wiped her mouth, she looked at him in astonishment.

"I know!" she said emphatically, "I put my life on hold yesterday – I was convinced that something was going to happen!"

David gave a little chuckle. "It was the sixth palindromic date so far this century in the UK format, all falling in Februarys, but yesterday was rare because it was a Global Palindrome Day – meaning it worked in both formats. That hasn't happened for 909 years – the last Global Palindrome Day was 11/11/1111."

"Wow!" exclaimed Eva, "You're the first person I know that's given any attention to numbers. Repeating numbers have had a major impact on my life for the past couple of years!"

"Really?" said David, "That sounds interesting."

Eva sipped her coffee, then placed the mug carefully on the table as she said quietly, "No, it's not interesting. You'll think I'm an irrational ninny if I tell you more."

David gave a hearty laugh. "Irrational ninny! That's not an expression I've heard for a long time!" and leaning forward he said earnestly, "I certainly wouldn't think anything of the sort! Everyone has their own reasons for everything they think or say and even if I don't agree with them I would never ridicule anything that anyone said – they all have their reasons."

Eva looked at her watch. "Gosh! Where has the time gone? I'll have to go." She hastily finished her coffee and gathered up her bag and as she went to wish him luck for the interview, David leaned across and laid his hand on her arm,

"Will you meet me at lunchtime?" he pleaded. "I can tell you how the interview went."

She hesitated. It had been so long since she went out with a man on anything other than a business lunch that she was aware of nervous flutters in her stomach. She looked into his velvety brown eyes and decided she could trust this man – didn't he also respect palindromic dates – and maybe even repeating numbers?

"I have a lunch break between one and two," she said, trying to sound casual as if it was simply a reporting back of a former meeting for him, "So….. shall we meet here? Mario does some nice paninis……… or we could go……"

"Here's fine," he said quickly, "I'll see you soon after one o'clock." He had stood up as she gathered her belongings, but he didn't move from the table and Eva walked out of the shop giving a farewell wave to Mario as she left.

As she continued on her way to the office, she wanted to giggle. She knew she was sporting a huge grin on her face and the cold wintry day had taken on a kind of brightness. How different she felt today compared to yesterday's bleak and depressing mindset. She imagined going to Fran's on the way home and telling her about this morning's encounter and how they would squeal like teenagers, then Fran would ask a hundred questions – how old was he? What did he look like? Did he smell nice? (That was important to Fran!) How was he dressed? Was he married…………..? *Oops! That's a good question! Didn't think of asking that……….but wait a minute………I'm reading something into this that might not even exist! He only wants to tell me about his interview, not have a relationship with me – it's all in my imagination!*

The conversation inside her head had the effect of throwing cold water on her. For a start, Fran wasn't there to tell about it, and there was nobody else she would want to share something like this with. And if she continued to weave a fantasy romance around quite an innocuous meeting between two people, then she deserved to be humiliated!

When she reached the office, her former grin had gone and she had to muster up some false enthusiasm to wish her colleagues a good morning. She had a few appointments in her diary – the first was a house viewing at nine-thirty then a shop site at eleven o'clock so she concentrated on checking her emails and gathering the property information before going out in the company car that was parked at the rear of the office. Trevor, who was the Surveyor, was the only staff member who used his own car.

The morning passed quickly and at twelve thirty Eva was back in the office completing her paperwork. Her colleague, Anita, asked if she wanted to come for a pizza, but Eva said, as nonchalantly as she could, that she was meeting someone.

"Oh?" said Anita, raising an eyebrow, "Anyone interesting?"

"Just a friend," said Eva, not looking up from her computer screen and trying to keep her breathing steady as her stomach fluttered irrationally.

When she arrived at Mario's, David was already there, at the same table that they'd sat at that morning. He was facing the door so he could see her as she walked in and his eyes lit up at once.

"Hi," he said smiling, leaning forward to pull the chair away from behind him and stand up with his hand holding his tie across his chest so that it didn't drop into the large coffee mug that stood in front of him. "Had a good morning?"

"Not too bad, quite busy," said Eva, feeling ridiculously pleased that he looked so delighted to see her. She liked his politeness and chivalry – the fact that he stood up as she walked to the table - it might be old-fashioned but it made her feel cherished. She unwound her scarf as she sat down across from him and Mario was beside her a few moments later, brandishing his lunchtime panini menu. Eva shrugged off her coat and giving a cursory glance at the menu said, "I'll have the chicken and mozzarella." It was her favourite.

"I'll have the same," said David as he handed the menu back to Mario with a smile. "Thank you, Mario."

"So, how did it go? The interview?" asked Eva, leaning towards him, keen to hear his news.

"I think I've done okay. I felt comfortable and could answer all of their questions. They said they'll make a decision today, so I should hopefully hear before the end of the day." He was nodding optimistically and Eva felt a genuine glow of pleasure for him.

"I'll keep my fingers crossed for you," said Eva. "Does your wife work? What does she do?" she asked, feigning innocence but pleased with the way she had slipped this important detail in so easily.

David looked blankly at her, then said, "My wife is dead."

"Oh, gosh, I'm so sorry," said Eva slightly shocked at how trite he had made this statement sound.

"Sorry, sorry! That sounded quite unfeeling, didn't it?" he said with a deep frown on his face. "But we'd lived apart for three years and we were halfway through our divorce when she died suddenly, five years ago. So, where I would have been a divorcee, I am now classed as a widower! Not that it matters, really, I've lived by myself for the last eight years." He sat back while Mario's young assistant brought their paninis, then leaned towards her and said, "How about you, have you got a husband – partner – significant other?"

Eva gave a small laugh. "No, nothing like that – I'm divorced, have been for the past ten years. I've a grown daughter and son. Have you got a family?"

"No," he said, "We never had children. I've nieces and nephews though, my sisters' children – two sisters, both with two children each, and they visit quite a lot."

They spent the next few minutes enjoying their paninis, then David asked her, "What you were saying this morning…… about putting your life on hold yesterday, what did you mean by it?"

Eva took time to swallow her food, then took a deep breath in. "A few years ago I started going through periods of waking up through the night always when the clock had repeating numbers on it – like 2:22 or 3:33 or 4:44, every night, always a repeating number and it freaked me out a bit. It would carry on for several nights, then stop for a while. Then I noticed that every time I had one of these 'episodes' it preceded an event that was either traumatic or upsetting in some way. So then it became almost like a prediction, to the point that I was scared to look at the clock once an episode began."

Eva was looking down at her panini, unwilling to look at him in case he was laughing at her, regretting saying so much so early on to someone she barely knew.

"That's pretty awful. I can understand how it can paralyse your thinking. Is that why yesterday's palindrome day had such an effect on you?" He was looking at her earnestly and when she did look up to meet his gaze she was gratified to see concern and understanding in his eyes. She nodded silently, picking little pieces from her panini and putting them slowly into her mouth.

"I suppose you've thought about swapping for an analogue clock?" he asked cautiously.

"I need a radio alarm – I wake up a lot through the night, but then have difficulty hearing an alarm when it's time to get up, so I use a radio alarm. I've tried everywhere but I can't find an electric radio-alarm clock with an analogue face – they're all digital." Eva was beginning to feel rather foolish as if she was making a big issue out of something trivial.

"Leave it with me! I should be able to source one for you! Can I have your phone number? I can let you know if I can get one." He was taking his phone out of his pocket as he was speaking and Eva nodded and recited her number and he keyed it in then rang her number. She took her phone out of her bag and he said, "That's my number, so you'll recognise it and not be scared to answer an unknown number on your phone."

She smiled at him and stored his number in her phone. "I'd better be getting back – I've quite a busy afternoon." She dropped her phone into her bag and took out her purse. David leaned across and laid his hand gently on her arm, saying,

"Please, let me get lunch. I'm sure you brought me luck in my interview – now I've got your number I can ring you and let you know if I was successful or not. If you're interested, I mean!"

"Of course I am! And thank you very much for lunch – you must let me do the honours one day."

"Let me see what I can do about your clock, and then we can arrange to meet up again……if you're willing?" He was looking at her with such hope in his eyes, she felt a warm glow and a strong feeling of positivity that she hadn't felt for many years.

"I'd like that," she said shyly, then turning to wave to Mario she made her way to the door and was pleased to notice he was following her out. As they got outside she spent a moment winding her scarf round her neck and buttoning up her coat and David shrugged on his overcoat, then he took her arm and said, "Let me walk to your office with you, then I'll continue on to an outlet I know that may have the item you require."

"Don't waste your day trying to find a clock – I'm sure you don't have much time off work, so you could enjoy the freedom of a day off!" But inside she was secretly pleased that he was taking her 'issue' seriously and trying to find a solution to make her life easier. She also enjoyed the feeling of her arm linked through his and his other hand lying gently across her hand. When they got to the office, she said goodbye to him and as she opened the door he said, "I'll ring you when I have it – or news of when I can get it!"

"Thank you," she said with a grateful smile as she slipped through the door, thankful that none of her colleagues were around to see her with him – she wanted to enjoy this time without anyone teasing her.

Throughout the day, every time she remembered David she felt a smile curl her mouth and her stomach flipped making her heart miss a beat. *Was this what yesterday was all about* she wondered? All her anguish over numbers – was it a message from a higher source? She certainly felt an awakening but she wasn't sure it was spiritual!

When her phone rang at four o'clock and she saw his name and number on the display, she hastily looked around to see who was in the office but relaxed when she saw Trevor and Anita at their computers and Louise attending to a client. She walked over to the large filing cabinet as she answered her phone and stood so that she was partially out of view but where she could watch the room to see if anyone was taking notice of her. She didn't want anyone making fun of her for how she had met David and how she had so easily agreed to meet with him for lunch on the same day – and now he was trying to purchase a particular clock for her…… and she hardly knew him!

She was shy as she spoke into her phone, saying "Hello David," and he said immediately, "I don't want to bother you at work, but can I meet you when you finish? I've managed to get what I think you need."

"Um, yes, that will be okay……. I finish at five-thirty." She felt a blush grow on her cheeks.

"I'll meet you outside your office – well, just down the road a bit so I don't look like I'm stalking you! Is that alright?"

She said it was and they ended the call, then she stood for a few moments clutching her phone to her chest. She had tickles of excitement inside her stomach and she tried to berate herself for behaving like a teenager but she couldn't wipe the smile off her face. This had never happened to her before - it had been ten years since she divorced Eddie and she hadn't had even one date with a man since then. She had focused her energies on raising her children and establishing a career for herself through on-line learning courses and evening classes at college to gain her Estate Agent Diploma.

By the time five-thirty arrived, Eva was waiting with her coat buttoned up and her scarf wrapped round her neck and her bag – the item that had introduced her to David - already hitched up onto her shoulder.

"You in a hurry tonight?" asked Trevor as he locked the filing cabinets and pulled the inner doors closed.

"Yes, I've something to do," mumbled Eva as she groped in her bag for her gloves.

They all trooped out of the office and Eva waited till the alarm had been set, furtively glancing around to see if she could see David, and there he was three buildings away, under a streetlight, holding an unbranded carrier bag in one hand and his briefcase in the other. She had a rush of guilt mixed with appreciation when she remembered he had spent the whole day in the city, firstly undergoing an interview this morning then spending the rest of the day shopping for something for her. She had never been treated so kindly or felt so valued.

She waved at her colleagues as they went in the opposite direction and she walked towards David, shyly fiddling with the strap of her bag on her shoulder. He grinned as he stepped towards her holding out the carrier bag.

"I think you'll like this – you were right in saying there's not many analogue radio alarm clocks, but I tracked this one down." He held the carrier bag open so she could see the box inside – it read '*3 in 1 - Lamp, Clock and Radio Alarm, lifetime guarantee, accurate to 1 second in 1 million years'* and showed a bright illustration of the item inside the box – a white lamp on top of a white-faced clock with black and green numerals and underneath a panel showing radio wavelengths.

"Ooh! That looks superb! Where on earth did you find that? It's lovely! It's got everything – I can dispose of my bedside lamp, I only need this one thing on my cabinet." She was truly taken aback at the clock and could picture it on her bedside cabinet and knew she would never again fear looking at the clock through the night. "I'm very grateful. How much do I owe you?"

David looked slightly embarrassed. "Would you consider accepting it as a gift? Please? You see, I got the job! I would like to celebrate by making this gift to you – you brought me luck, so it's my way of saying thank you!"

"Congratulations! Well done on getting the job! But it doesn't seem right somehow – you should be getting the treat, not me."

"Well……….. I've a suggestion – do you have to rush off home?" Eva shook her head slowly, her lips slightly pursed.

"Well," continued David, "If you feel awkward accepting this as a gift – you could take us both for a meal – I noticed a nice little Italian Restaurant two streets away that's open from five o'clock!"

Eva's eyes widened. "I'm sure that wouldn't cover the cost of this clock," she said.

"I could have steak, to make you feel better," he countered., making Eva laugh.

"Well, if you're sure……" she said.

"Off we go, then," he said, sliding the carrier bag into the hand that was carrying his briefcase then holding his free arm out and bent at an angle, he urged her to slide her arm through the crook of his arm, which she happily did.

Once they were seated in the restaurant and all bags were on the floor, he answered her questions about where he'd managed to purchase the clock radio from and she inwardly gasped! It was a shop she would never have gone in because of the cost of the range of their goods and wondered exactly how much he had paid for it.

He told her about the phone call he'd received offering him the job, how it would enhance his career and as it was a step up the career ladder it also meant a big salary increase.

They ordered the food and chatted easily, telling each other various things about their lives and then he asked Eva more about her number phobia.

"I don't think it's a phobia as such, not like arithmophobia," she told him, then laughed at his surprised look. "Yes, I Googled it! I mean it's not ALL numbers that I'm scared of – it's just the time on a digital clock when they're repeating numbers. Although I suppose it IS a fear of specific numbers so it does signify a phobia! Anyway, it's an anxiety disorder, I know that much. A few friends have said if it was such a fear I would have stopped using a digital alarm clock – but like I said before – I couldn't find an analogue alarm clock-radio and I never wake to the sound of normal alarms."

"Well, hopefully, you won't have to suffer any more!" said David with a smile. "However, you will have to stay in touch with me to ensure that the problem is solved!"

"I don't think that will be a hardship," said Eva coyly and his smile deepened.

When their meal was finished and the waiter brought the bill which he placed nearer to David than to Eva, she stretched across to pick up the wallet that held the bill, but David picked it up first and held it to his chest.

Eva looked up at him and he grimaced. "I'm so sorry, but it goes against every fibre of my being – I asked you to dine with me, I'm afraid I can't let you pay!"

"But that was the agreement!" protested Eva, "To pay for the clock!"

"Please," David implored, "Please accept the clock as a gift, and allow me the privilege of taking you to dinner. I'm old-fashioned, I know, but please indulge me!"

Eva sighed. "Well, I'm very grateful, for both the clock and the meal. But you must allow me to return the deed one day."

"Most certainly!" said David, emphatically, "Does that mean you'll come out with me again?" He had a huge grin on his face and a hopeful look in his eyes.

"I must confess," said Eva leaning forward, "This is the first time I've been out with a man since my divorce ten years ago. I'm a bit rusty on how to behave."

"Actually, it's the same for me – I haven't dated anyone since my wife and I separated eight years ago. I never met anyone I was remotely interested in going out with. Until you hit me with your handbag, that is!" He laughed and Eva joined in, but looked suitably embarrassed.

"I was quite mortified when that happened – Gosh! Was it only this morning? I feel as if I've known you forever."

"Me too," he said and gently laid his hand on her hand that was on the table. "Now, we'd better walk to the bus-station. I've no idea what time the buses are – I usually drive to work."

"I don't know what time they are on an evening – I think the service times change after six o'clock," replied Eva.

David handed his card to the waiter to pay for the meal, quickly keying his number into the machine the waiter held out to him and stood up to help Eva into her coat. Then, when they were both protected against the elements, he picked up the carrier bag and his briefcase then tucked her hand through his arm and they headed outside.

They were fortunate to get a bus after only a few minutes standing in the bus queue and they both turned and looked at each other when they reached the place on the bus where they had first met – when her bag had hit him in the face.

"I think we can say this is our seat," he said laughingly and as Eva gave a rueful grimace, he whispered , "Don't be sorry – it was the best piece of luck I've ever had. Well worth the pain!"

When they were seated and the bus pulled away, David said, "Will you ring me tomorrow and tell me whether you like the clock - and more importantly – whether it helped rid you of your fear of looking at the time?"

"Of course I will. And thank you again, David, for the clock and the meal and for giving up your free afternoon to find the clock for me. I haven't been spoilt like this – ever!" Eva squeezed his arm as she said this and was then overcome with embarrassment when she remembered she'd only met him this morning and yet here she was acting as though they were old friends.

David must have read her mind because he laid his hand on hers and said, "I can hardly believe we've just met today – I feel as though you've always been in my life! Isn't it strange? If somebody else was telling me they'd become so close to someone within a few hours of meeting, I'd tell them they were a fool! But it's true – it's like we were meant to meet."

Eva smiled contentedly. She couldn't remember ever being so happy – not a giddy happy like a teenager, but a deep, fulfilled happiness that she felt secure in. She had the feeling that she could tell David anything about her insecurities and her fears and he would listen and understand and help her overcome them.

As the bus neared her stop, he got up to let her out of the seat and as she stood up next to him, she quickly reached up and kissed him on the cheek and said, "Thank you again. I'll ring you tomorrow. Goodnight."

As she stepped down from the bus her joy and confidence was soaring. *She* had kissed *him! She* initiated it! She felt absolutely in control and this made her feel powerful! She hugged the carrier bag to her chest and waved at him as the bus glided past, the interior lights shining brightly against the dark of the night.

She looked up at the night sky and was filled with a new sense of purpose and elation and she knew the rest of her life was going to be wonderful.

*****

The Message.

Celia drummed her fingertips on the top of the desk as she contemplated the Chair's report for Thursday's meeting. She needed to get a message across to the residents and wider community about the vandalism that was currently happening on a regular occurrence in the grounds and gardens. The Committee, when they met last week, had viewed the CCTV footage that had captured the actions of four youths playing in the landscaped gardens around the Victorian buildings, leaping from one seat to another and overturning the stone ornaments and statues. The images were too far away to distinguish any features and they were all dressed in similar clothing – hoodies in varying shades of grey, according to the black and white footage, and by their stature would probably be around fourteen or fifteen years old.

She was trying to somehow find the right words to describe the disappointment that she felt whenever she came across broken garden ornaments or graffiti-covered walls and statues and to get the point across to the residents that it was more than likely the work of someone that they knew, possibly even a member of their own family! She needed to say this

without alienating the community and causing them to be
defensive and hostile. She doubted whether the youngsters
themselves would be at the meeting – she could probably
count on one hand the number of youths that attended the
Community meetings although they had opened up the
meetings for whole families so that nobody could say they
couldn't come because they didn't have child-care. The
meetings were popular and usually quite well attended, more
so in the summer than the winter, but that was to be expected.

Celia regularly visited the Parent and Toddler Group in
the Community Centre and she went to the youth Club twice a
week hoping to make a connection with the young teenagers.
Last night when she was there she had carefully scrutinised all
the boys and had a bit of an inkling who may be responsible
for the vandalism, but obviously with no proof she couldn't do
anything. She had sat down with a small group of girls who
were not involved with any of the games and tried her best to
start a discussion around evening activities asking them what
kind of things they usually did and the kinds of things she did
as a child herself. As she suspected might happen, a few
others drifted over when they saw the girls laughing and
talking animatedly. Gradually the group expanded and one or
two of the boys wandered over, so Celia took the opportunity
to casually raise the subject of how distressed she'd been to

find the vandalism in the gardens and graffiti on the outside walls of the garage block near to the office.

"Well, I'm actually hoping that it was done by people rather than……….." Then she shook her head and stood up. "Forget what I just said," she told them as they all stared at her wide-eyed. Celia had surprised herself by what she'd said but the tiniest seed of an idea had come into her head and before she could make it into any kind of a plan, the words had seeped out.

"What do you mean?" asked Linzi Baker, a thirteen year old with five younger siblings at home who loved to come to the Youth Club as it was the only opportunity she had of having some time without a couple of them trailing after her. She looked slightly worried at Celia's words.

"Nothing," mumbled Celia, "I shouldn't have said anything! Forget it."

Linzi grabbed the arm of her friend Sadie and they strutted across the floor towards the pool table where they hovered hoping to catch the eye of Max Tillotson, a fourteen year old who was fancied by most of the girls in the club. He was tall and broad-shouldered, due partly to the fact that he played rugby, but when he was with his father it was obvious where he got his physique from – his dad was a Personal Trainer at the Gym and set great store by physical fitness.

When the club was finished and the youngsters had noisily left, Celia stayed to help Elaine and Tom to clear up and put the equipment back in the large storage cupboards so that the room was ready to be set out for the next activity. While they were working they were talking about the recent vandalism and Tom had said he thought it was kids who lived in the nearby council estate and who attended the club, but Celia had said she thought the main culprits were a couple of the lads who lived in the complex.

Willoughby Place was a housing complex that had been created from the dilapidated buildings of an old Victorian Hospital and Sanitorium over twenty-five years ago and which had stood empty for many decades before it was purchased by a Housing Association in 1959. It took three years to renovate and re-build and it could accommodate a community of between 600 and 800 residents in a total of 245 dwellings in a mix of 1, 2 and 3 bedroomed houses and flats. Celia had come to live here three years ago when she downsized from her family home after her daughter and son had left home to live independently and start their own families and she managed to get a lovely one-bedroomed property in Willoughby Place. She had decided to go into rented property because she had faced so many issues of maintenance and major repairs in the family home over the last twelve years as a widow that she decided to sell and share the money with her son and daughter to help them while they were starting out in life and more likely to need the financial help. They were against it at first but she was adamant that she wanted to spend her remaining years stress free and in relevant comfort.

The buildings were built on a hill in a very large rectangle surrounding a central garden but because of the lie of the land it was multi-layered and several years ago had been landscaped by the Gardening Group overseen by Geoff Wilson, a resident and retired landscape gardener. The statues and garden ornaments were an eclectic mix of concrete animals made by Sam Eldon who lived on the nearby estate and made garden ornaments to sell to raise money for a charity he was involved in, along with various figures that had been purchased from garden centres including stone plinths that held large ceramic pots of plants and flowers. The residents had held fund-raising events to purchase them, but some residents bought their own and placed them in the gardens themselves, particularly memorial figures for a loved one they had lost.

On the side of the complex where most of the family homes were there was a substantial play area for the children. Part of the apparatus was built into the hillside so that the natural environment was used to its advantage. To one side of the large playground was an enclosed smaller play area for younger children with some seating for parents. The playground was well used and maintained voluntarily by a group of parents who did a good job of checking the equipment and keeping the ground free from litter, although it was a constant source of bickering amongst the residents. This was because a group of youngsters would normally congregate there on an evening and next morning there would be crisp packets and sweet wrappers blowing about and the parents who picked up the litter always moaned about 'other people's kids' being litter-louts.

In 1962 when Willoughby Place was first created it was a flagship project for the Housing Association and received many accolades, but as times and residents changed the ethos was gradually lost and by the mid eighties the Housing Association decided to embark on partial Tenant Management. They had devolved some of the everyday running of the complex to a management committee but their prime function was to interview prospective new tenants and give their feedback to the Lettings manager of the Association who used this information to accept or reject applications. The only impediment to this working successfully was that by law Housing Associations had to accept a percentage of people from the Council's Homeless list, therefore In these cases the Tenant Management Lettings Committee still interviewed these applicants but it was in an advisory capacity and they could not reject them.

One of the criteria when a new person took up residence was that everyone was expected to share their skills to create a caring community. They wanted tenants to take responsibility for the general cleanliness and tidiness of the community areas. They had to agree to help to keep the environment in good condition, or run activities for children, young people or elderly residents as well as the wider community in the Community Centre that was situated in one corner of the huge rectangle on the upper level of the complex. There was always a steady core group of about twenty-five residents who were heavily involved in various working parties across the area and each group met every couple of weeks in the Community Centre office. The Housing Association were satisfied with the system in Willoughby Place and encouraged it to continue.

Celia was very happy living here. She had been elected as Chair of the Tenants Association at the beginning of the previous year and was in post for a period of three years before elections would take place again. She had thoroughly enjoyed the position as it gave her a sense of purpose since she retired from work and she had developed many friendships and was a popular figure as she walked around the complex.

Bringing herself back to the present, she tried once more to get down on paper a way of presenting the problems in a way that wouldn't start a barrage of animosity and acerbic comments from some of the members. She knew that Joseph Lyman, an elderly retired bachelor who had lived there for eleven years, would immediately say it was the teenagers on the complex encouraging others from the council estate nearby – those parents who had no interest in keeping the area clean, they had their rent paid for them and expected everything to be done for them, they never kept their children under control – too busy smoking and drinking - and so on, till he would be silenced by an uproar from several of the tenants who shouted him down and yelling that he was a mealy-mouthed snob who hated children and had no right insulting people the way he did……….Celia groaned, holding her head in her hands, knowing the direction the meeting was likely to go in.

She quickly dropped her hands as the office door opened and Matthew Handley came in. He was the Treasurer on the Committee and he smiled widely when he saw Celia sitting at the desk in front of the window overlooking the entrance to Willoughby Place.

"Good morning," he said, "Are you busy?"

"Well…… I should be! I'm doing the Chair's report for the meeting," replied Celia, "I'm trying to think of a way I can say something about the recent vandalism without starting a verbal conflict between the parents and the childless and those having sly digs at the tenants accepted from the homeless list! You know who I mean………..he's bound to start it off!"

"Well, it does need to be addressed – we can't just ignore it," said Matthew.

"I know! And that's why I'm struggling! I want to get the message across without starting a blame war!" Celia sighed.

Matthew opened the filing cabinet and took out the ledgers and financial records and took them over to the other desk in the office.

"Accounts are looking good," he said.

"Just as well," mumbled Celia, "We'll need a bit of expenditure to put the damage right!"

Matthew gave a little chuckle. "Don't be glum, Celia," he said, "Geoff's had a look and he says we've enough graffiti remover in the store and he's already righted all the statues and ornaments. I'll help him later today with cleaning off the graffiti. Have you seen it, by the way?"

"Of course I have! Sharon Buckle told me straight away – she saw it first thing when she went for her early morning walk around the gardens! She was furious!"

"Actually, whoever has done it has got some artistic potential!" said Matthew nodding his head thoughtfully.

"For goodness sake! Don't be encouraging them!" said Celia, "Otherwise every surface will be covered in graffiti!"

"Well, aerosol cans cost money, so it has to be someone who can afford to buy them………" said Matthew still deep in thought. "Any ideas from the youth club?"

"No, not really," Celia said as she stood up and stretched. "It might have helped if we'd seen the culprit on the CCTV footage but the camera only covers the gardens and doesn't cover that part of the building. We might need another camera."

Matthew nodded pensively then was silent as he worked on the financial report for the meeting, and Celia sat back down and picked up her pen and tried again to get some words down on paper. When she saw Matthew put his pen down and sit back she said hesitantly, "Can I run something past you, Matthew?"

"Fire away!" said Matthew.

"Well……..last night when I was in the youth club……..I kind of………..said a few words……..I wanted to hint …….

that we might have a ghost…….that the gardens might be haunted!" Celia grimaced.

"Haunted? But why?" asked Matthew.

"Well, my idea was that if they started to believe that there was a ….ghost…… or apparition of some kind………prowling the grounds, they might stay out of the gardens."

Matthew gave a chuckle. "How did they take the news?"

"Well I didn't actually say it was haunted – I just put the idea out that ……….well, I said I hoped it was a person and not…………." She hunched up her shoulders with her hands spread out. "Then I said to forget I'd said anything!"

"And were they curious and pressed you for more?" asked Matthew.

"A bit………..but I wanted to just put the idea out there to start with. I was thinking of hinting a bit more next time, then eventually they'll urge me to give the full story and I can create a wandering spirit who is angry because his wife was in the sanitorium against his wishes and he walks the grounds looking for her…………..or something?" Celia looked expectantly at Matthew.

"And what if someone takes it to the press?" laughed Matthew, "Or asks to have the place tested for paranormal activity? They'd soon find out there's nothing supernatural about this place."

"How likely is that? Can you imagine the press being remotely interested?" Celia asked him, feeling more confident about her story. "If we got the youngsters to believe it, they might stop being destructive in the gardens!"

Matthew didn't answer. He knew Celia of old – they'd been colleagues for a couple of years about fifteen years ago when they were both involved in the setting up of a new City Centre project dealing with runaway kids and he knew that once Celia set her mind to something, she usually found a way of carrying it out. He and his wife were already living in Willoughby Place when Celia arrived and they were both equally happy to renew their acquaintance with her. She had been a great source of comfort to him when his wife, Sally, passed away nineteen months ago.

Matthew put the ledgers back into the filing cabinet and locked it, then picking up the papers from the desk, he told her he was going home, unless she wanted him to stay and help her with her report.

"No, I'm not getting anywhere – I'm not in the right frame of mind," decided Celia, "I'll come back to it later. I'll walk over with you." She picked up her notebook and pen and thrust them into her bag then came out of the office with Matthew, locking the door behind them.

Later that day, Celia made sure she was around the main entrance road coming into Willoughby Place, where she knew the bus dropped the teenagers coming home from the high school. She had busied herself dead-heading the rose bushes and doing a bit of weeding in the large planters that adorned the verges either side of the road.

Sadie, Linzi, Michelle and Bethany were walking arm-in-arm taking up the entire pavement and Linzi on the end constantly hopping up and down from the kerb onto the road as they giggled and laughed on their way home.

"Hello, girls, " said Celia, "Had a good day?"

"Yes, thanks," said Bethany, "That looks nice, Celia, you've done a good job."

"Thank you, Bethany, do you like gardening?" asked Celia, hoping to get them to stay and chat.

"Nah," said Bethany, "But I like to see the planters looking neat."

"Yes, me too," nodded Celia looking thoughtful.

"Celia……..you know last night when you said………"
began Sadie, causing Celia's heart to beat a bit faster, "When
you said you hoped it was a person who had caused the
damage?………...What did you mean?…………….What else
could it be?……….. An animal?" Sadie's brows were knitted
together in concern.

From the corner of her eye, Celia could see Max
Tillotson and Luke Somerby turning into the road, huge
backpacks carried on one shoulder causing them to stoop
slightly forward. She pretended to look round to see if anyone
could hear and the girls edged in closer.

"Well, I shouldn't really be telling you this, but there's a
story that there's a spirit that walks the grounds here……….."
She looked around again, mainly to see how close Max and
Luke were. "You know this place originally was a Sanatorium?
Well, the story is that in 1888 – exactly a hundred years ago -
a young woman was taken in suffering from scarlet fever
which was one of the epidemics of that century. Her husband
– who loved her a great deal - created the gardens for her to
see from her window and where he would work from morning
till night so that every time she looked out she could see him."
The girls all uttered "oohs" and "aahs" - sounds of sympathy
and envy for such romantic love.

Celia carried on, noticing that Max and Luke had joined the group and were listening in. "In those days, Sanatoriums mainly housed the insane, but two of the wings…….…..." Celia gestured to the lower half of the complex, "They were modified to care for the sufferers of scarlet fever. One day when the husband was sitting in the garden, as usual, he noticed that there seemed to be a lot of commotion coming from the inside of the building." Celia had warmed to her theme now and was thoroughly enjoying making up this tale. "Well, to cut a long story short, one of the insane inmates had escaped and had hidden in the scarlet fever ward. When he was found, he was discovered to be suffering from typhus – which was a plague-like illness - and because of the young woman's already weakened condition, she contracted the deadly disease and soon afterwards she died. The husband was beside himself with grief and within a year, he too had died. And it's said that his spirit still walks the earth because of the anger and grief he carried when he died – he is unable to pass to the other side."

There was a deep silence as all six of the young people contemplated in awe what Celia had told them.

"Oh, how sad," said Linzi finally, "So that's what you meant when you said………

"I didn't know whether it was his spirit becoming angry and being able to ………..do things, like poltergeists do………… or whether he's trying to find her………I mean, I don't know how things like that work………" Celia deliberately made herself sound vague in case their questions became too deep. "Or it could simply be vandals!" she said, shaking her head sadly.

"Gosh!" said Sadie, "I won't be going down there in the dark, that's for sure!"

"Me neither!" said Bethany and Linzi and Michelle nodded their assent.

Celia noticed that Max and Luke didn't comment, but Max nudged Luke and they walked around the girls and sauntered off towards home their hands deep in their pockets. The girls said goodbye to Celia and hastened after the boys and Celia watched them all as they walked up the path, a small smile on her face. She'd fed their imaginations and now it was up to them to get the message to the other teens on the complex. She couldn't help but give a little inward chuckle when she thought about how easily the story had poured from her mouth.

On Thursday evening Celia walked into the Community Centre meeting room and unfurled the sheet of flipchart paper she carried and pinned it to the board. This showed the agenda for the meeting and she studied it when she took a step back to make sure the secretary hadn't forgotten anything. Margaret, the Tenants Association secretary, had said she would be slightly late as her husband was late home from work and she needed him to look after the children who she thought were too young to be out later than their scheduled bedtime of seven o'clock.

Celia had managed to get her report done and had decided she was not going to labour the point of the vandalism as it was all fixed now thanks to the Gardening group. She knew it would have to be reported, but she didn't want to give Joseph the chance of a long tirade of insults, so she had taken the option of talking about the strengths of the working parties and community groups and how they can respond easily to the kind of problems that *all* housing complexes suffer from, particularly those where there was mixed housing of family and single person properties.

One of the agenda items was the request by her for funds to pay for an artist to come into the Community Centre to do an introductory session to see how many people would like to take up art as a hobby. She had thought about what Matthew had said about the graffiti showing potential and had telephoned the local college who had an extensive art department and had enquired about different types of art, traditional, abstract, still-life, then hesitantly mentioned graffiti and the college tutor said eagerly that street art was becoming very popular and a good idea where graffiti was an issue.

Celia was quite excited at the prospect and if the Community funds would cover it, she was sure this would resolve the graffiti problems. When she raised the item she wasn't going to go into detail about the street art. This would be raised with the tutor once it was booked.

A staff member from the Housing Association would also attend the meeting. This was part of the agreement when they negotiated the terms and conditions of partial Tenant Management of the complex. Sometimes it was Steve, the Housing Manager, and sometimes it was Malcolm, head of the repairs team but everyone got along well and this was an opportunity to resolve any repair issues and get several jobs done at the same time.

As people started to drift in, laughing and joking with each other, Celia went into the kitchen to see if Audrey and Adrian needed any help making teas and coffees, but it was all under hand. Looking around she gave a sigh of contentment and blessed the day she had decided to take up a tenancy in this complex, much against her family's wishes. They hadn't understood her desire to go into rented property and 'pour money down the sink each month paying rent'. But Celia stood firm and was glad she did – she had a deep sense of belonging living here and when her son and daughter visited and brought their young children, they were appeased when they saw how nice the complex was and how many friends their mum had made and that they didn't have to worry about her feeling lonely.

The meeting went extremely well and afterwards when she was talking to Malcolm and Matthew, she confessed that she had glossed over the graffiti issue because of the predicted outcome and when Matthew had said the graffiti artist was probably very talented, it had led her to investigate at the local college for an art tutor and possibly art classes of various kinds. Malcolm had said it was an excellent idea and that he would have a word with Steve, the Housing Manager, and they could possibly release some funds from the Housing Association's Community Fund to pay the cost, then the Tenants Association own funds wouldn't suffer as all their money came from the fund-raising that they did from Bingo, Fayres and Jumble sales and such-like.

On her way back home, Celia walked through the gardens to get to her house and as it was a balmy September evening she sat a while on one of the seats that they had strategically placed around the multi-levelled garden area. She loved this garden. Geoff and his band of gardener volunteers spent many hours weeding and planting and keeping the area immaculate which it was why it was so tragic when the ornaments and figurines were thrown about or overturned. There were solar lights of all shapes and sizes dotted around that the residents had added over the years and the whole area was tranquil and picturesque.

She sat quietly, hearing distant voices as people from the meeting made their way home or stood talking outside their houses and finally it was all still and peaceful. The sky was clear and she looked up and could see hundreds of stars twinkling in the sky and she felt her throat tighten as she remembered how she and her husband, Paul, would often sit in their own garden looking at the stars and talking about anything and everything. She still missed him, even after all this time – twelve years had gone by since he was tragically killed in a road accident two days after his fifty-fifth birthday. She had never forgiven the drunk driver that was behind the wheel that crashed head-on into Paul's car, even though he also had died she was of the mind that he deserved it, but Paul hadn't!

She took a deep breath in to steady her emotions and blinked rapidly to clear her eyes of unshed tears, when she heard footsteps. It was Matthew, slowly walking towards her deep in thought and he gave a slight start when he saw her sitting quietly.

"Oh, Celia, you startled me! Are you okay?" he asked.

"Yes, I'm fine. Just enjoying the peace and tranquillity of the garden. I love it here."

"Me too," said Matthew and Celia moved along the seat to allow room for him to sit next to her and they both sat in companionable silence. After a few moments. Celia gave a little giggle and Matthew turned to look at her.

"Do you know what I've done, Matthew?" she asked and when his eyebrows shot up enquiringly, she gave another self-conscious giggle and said, "I've told the youth club girls a story about the 'ghost' that walks these gardens!" Matthew gave a hearty laugh and then Celia proceeded to tell him what she had told the girls and how she hoped they would spread the word amongst the others, especially as most of them had said that they would definitely not be walking in the gardens in the dark.

"What a tragic tale, but very romantic!" said Matthew, "You've a definite talent there, Celia, you could be a novelist!"

"I haven't got the patience to write it down," she said, "But I admit I did enjoy making it up on the spot! I don't even know where it came from!"

"Well, I suppose the end justifies the means if it works. We'll just have to keep the story going. That might be difficult with those who've lived her for many years – they'll wonder why this story has suddenly emerged," said Matthew thoughtfully. "Or they might just poo-poo the tale and ignore it."

Celia nodded then changing the subject she said, "That was a good offer from Malcolm – well, if Steve agrees to help pay for the art tutor – don't you think?" Celia turned to Matthew. "I thought about what you said about potential talent and so I rang the college and spoke to the art department and they sound really keen to do a project here."

"Yes, it's really good news! I was a bit taken aback when you brought it up, considering the fact that you weren't that keen when I first mentioned it……..but I know you, Celia, and I know that's how you work. But if the college are interested and the Housing Association are keen, we just have to get the community on board, especially the graffiti artistes, without there being internal conflict amongst them all!"

"Well, I thought we'd have open meetings for art classes and the 'street art' as they call it, can be carried out in the youth club session. I can't see many older residents wanting to know about graffiti as an art!" Celia and Matthew chuckled together, imagining how residents like Joseph Lyman would react.

Celia stood up and stretched her back. "I'm going to get off home now," she said.

"I'll walk with you," said Matthew, "I only came out for a brief walk as it was such a lovely night."

"Would you like to come to mine for a coffee ……. or a cup of cocoa?" asked Celia.

"Well, I live nearer, so do you want to come to mine?" asked Matthew.

"Have you got cocoa?" asked Celia, pursing her lips.

"Of course," said Matthew, "Doesn't every self-respecting pensioner?"

The next night at the youth club, the girls crowded round Celia as soon as she came into the room, pressing her for more details about 'the ghost'.

"I don't know any more than I've told you," said Celia, feeling a glow of pleasure that they were taking it seriously.

"Have you ever seen anything?" asked Sarah Fenwick, a ten-year-old who lived on the nearby estate and who came every Friday with her eight year old sister and who had both heard the story and were now scared of going into the gardens in the dark.

"No, I haven't," admitted Celia,

"Well, who has?" demanded Michelle Cawley.

"Somebody must have for the story to have started," reasoned Celia, "But I don't know……… I just know it scares me when things get thrown about or damaged ……….as if it was done in anger……...."

"Well I know for a fact it was Tony Gibson and Terry Dunn that did the last trashing," said Sadie Smith in a conspiratorial low voice.

Celia felt a glow of pleasure. Aha! Success! She'd had the vandals identified! But she knew they would deny it if they were confronted and their parents would say it wasn't their boys if she visited and told them. But at least her ploy had brought results.

"Mmm," said Celia thoughtfully, "Perhaps they shouldn't anger the ghost – he might get upset that his garden is being disrespected. I've heard some awful things that have happened to people who have angered a wandering spirit…………" She decided to change the subject before she got into deep water – she had planted the story, it was up to them now to spread the message. She began to talk about the artist that they were going to bring into the Centre and the kind of art they preferred. She didn't mention the street art – she would keep that little gem for another day and perhaps find out who the graffiti artist was as a result!

When the youth club was finished and they had all left, she stayed back as usual to help Elaine and Tom clear away. Tom made them all a cup of tea when it was all tidy and they sat in the kitchen drinking it and chatting about the night. Elaine asked Celia if she'd heard the latest that the girls were on about – a ghost that walks the gardens?

Celia contemplated confiding in Elaine and Tom but decided against it. If she told many people that she'd made it up, then it might eventually get back to the youngsters – and there would be some adults who were totally against telling 'stories', or lies, to young people, and for moment or two Celia felt a surge of guilt. She was going against every rule in the book as far as being open and honest with children and young people went, but then smothered these feelings of guilt – didn't Matthew agree that the end justifies the means?

She told Elaine that she'd heard them talking but then changed the subject to talk about other things, not wanting to pursue the ghost story. Elaine was happy to chat about the decorating she was doing in her house and the colour themes she had planned to go with the new lounge furniture she had seen that she was thinking of buying. Celia encouraged her to talk as it took her away from the ghost story.

Saturday was a beautiful sunny day and Celia went shopping in town and spent the morning browsing the shops before going for some lunch then finally going for her two-thirty hairdresser's appointment. When she got home she was quite tired out, so when she had put away the various items that she had bought in town she took her garden chair out into her small, neat garden at the back of her house and sat dozing in the late afternoon sun. When the sun moved behind the rooftops, the temperature dropped and the chill woke her up. She shuddered and pulled her cardigan around her and made her way indoors.

There was a Bingo session at the Community Centre that night so she decided to go. She wasn't particularly fond of Bingo, but every so often she went so that she could help with the fund-raising and she could also have a chat with other people.

She got there about ten minutes before it was due to start and as soon as she walked through the door she could feel a buzz in the air. As she looked around she could see all the clusters of people around each table talking animatedly and she asked Kathleen who was selling the bingo tickets what was going on.

"Oh, they're all talking about this ghost that's supposed to be wandering around the garden area..........I've never

seen anything," Kathleen said and sniffed disdainfully. Celia
had a flush of guilt but said nothing and just picked up her
tickets and made her way to a table that had a spare seat at it.
As she sat down, Maggie Fulton grabbed her arm.

"Have you ever seen the ghost, Celia," she asked, "I
don't know who it's a ghost of – somebody from last
century……...or something. I don't know why he's just started
haunting the place now!" Maggie's eyes were wide in eager
anticipation of gossip.

"I've not seen anything – but I've ………had
feelings……...you know? When I've been sitting there………..."
Celia felt that she ought to weave a bit more into the story
she'd invented – it wasn't hurting anyone. "Perhaps he's upset
at the vandalism ………..or perhaps it was him that did the
vandalising?"

"No! I think he's angry! I bet that's what it is! Carrie!"
Maggie turned to the table behind her. "Carrie, Celia thinks
it's because of the vandalism in the gardens – it's started the
hauntings!"

"Oh my! I'm going to tell my kids to keep well away –
not that I think mine had anything to do with it, " said Carrie,
"But I don't want them getting freaked out!" Carrie passed this
on to the rest of the people at her table and most of them
agreed it was best not to go in the dark, then they passed it on

to a few of the others on the next table who also reiterated what Carrie had said. A few of the residents who had lived at Willoughby Place for many years snorted derisively and said it was rubbish but they were in the minority. Celia noticed that Tony Gibson and Terry Dunn's mothers were both there who also said something but Celia was too far away to hear what they'd said – she just hoped they were saying they would get the message to their boys as well. She felt a little smirk curl up the sides of her mouth as she realised how quickly something could rage like a wildfire round a small community. She just prayed that what Matthew said was right – the end would justify the means!

When she got home after the Bingo session she had a feeling of unrest. She decided to have a walk down to the gardens again – maybe take a flask of cocoa and sip it while she sat on the seat. As she filled the flask the wondered about knocking on Matthew's door and asking him if he wanted to come, so she popped two cups into the bag with the flask. As an afterthought she added a packet of digestive biscuits.

Approaching Matthew's house she had second thoughts. It was about quarter-past nine and she wondered if asking Matthew to come was a bit forward of her. She didn't want him to think she had designs on him or anything………she hesitated, then imagined if he had approached her, what would she think? Her initial reaction would be one of wariness and although she probably would go, she would be quite cautious, wondering if there may be romantic inclinations.

Oh, bother it! she said to herself. *It's not worth losing a friend! Just go yourself, Celia, that's what you'd first planned, more cocoa for you!*

She walked quickly past Matthew's door and turned down the path towards the gardens. She'd started with a headache and hoped the cool night air would take it away. When she got into the garden area it was quiet and tranquil just as she expected it to be and she got to the seat where she and Matthew had sat on Thursday night.

She sat breathing deeply in the night air, feeling her body relaxing and hoping the release of tension would reach her head. After a few minutes she opened the flask and poured herself a cup of cocoa and sat sipping the hot, sweet liquid with genuine pleasure. She could hear distant sounds, voices and slight strains of music, but they were so far away and were comforting.

She had a sudden thought – what if the boys came back tonight to do a bit of damage to prove they weren't scared of a ghost? What would she do? She wasn't afraid of them hurting her – she didn't think for one minute they would do that, but how would she handle the situation? *They probably wouldn't do anything simply because you're here – they won't do it in front of you,* she told herself, and was consoled by that thought.

She finished her cocoa and decided against having a second cup – she felt a bit sick and the headache was getting worse so she put the flask away and sat breathing deeply in the cool night air. September had been a lovely month, very warm and not many rainy days. She'd enjoyed the late summer and had had a couple of trips away early on in the month, one weekend in the Lake District and one midweek break to Barcelona with a friend she'd had since college days. She was very satisfied with her life – no stress, no money issues, yes, life was good.

She suddenly became aware of the temperature dropping and she shivered pulling her coat collar up. Then, in the top corner of the garden she became aware of a shadow that seemed to be growing bigger and moving down over the bushes and around the planters and she felt her pulse quicken. What could it be? The shadow seemed to take a shape, but then reformed into something else, but then rise up and become darker and denser. She felt the hairs on the back of her neck stand up and shivers went down her spine, but then the shadow took a definite shape – the shape of a person, and as she stared it took the form of a man, all the while travelling slowly towards her.

Was this the ghost? Was this the man she had invented? She tried to make sense of what she was seeing, but her mind seemed dulled and confused.

You're not real! her mind cried out, *I made you up! You can't exist.*

As the apparition got closer, her heart suddenly lurched inside her cheat – she could make out features now, a kind face, deep and twinkling eyes and a smile that could melt her heart – and often had. It was Paul! Her Paul, her beloved husband who had died twelve years before, but now he was here, coming towards her holding out his hand to her. She couldn't move! She wanted to run to him, throw herself at him, feel his strong arms around her, protecting her, cherishing her as they had for the thirty-four years they were married. She felt her senses reeling and she held out her hands to him. He came towards her and as a sudden blinding flash of light exploded in her head she felt his arms around her and joy filled every pore of her being and then there was nothing, nothing except love.

The next morning Sharon Buckle was doing her power walk around the complex and went through the gardens as she always did. As she rounded the lower garden she saw something on the seat – a coat, or a bundle of clothes and as she approached she saw it was a person.

With a racing heart she gradually approached the seat. She felt the blood drain from her face as she saw it was Celia, slumped on the seat. She hesitantly reached out and touched her hand but it was ice cold. With a whimper of fear, Sharon turned and fled, running madly back along the path towards the houses. As she got to the top of the path the first house she saw with signs of life was Matthew's and she ran up and pounded on his door.

Moments later Matthew pulled the door open and his jaw dropped as he saw the fear and panic on Sharon's face and her mouth working furiously trying to get words out.

"It's Celia!" she finally croaked, "In the gardens, on the seat, I think she's……. I think she's…….. Ooh! Get an ambulance!"

"Oh, my God!" gasped Matthew and he turned and rushed back into his house and grabbed the telephone, shouting for Sharon to come inside. She was slumped in the doorframe and managed to haul herself across the threshold and flop down on the nearest chair, whimpering all the while.

Matthew gave the brief details to the emergency services and his address and once he was sure that help was on the way he put the phone back on the cradle then crouched down in front of Sharon. She was making soft moaning sounds and shaking her head so Matthew went to the kitchen and brought her a glass of water, but then as he guessed she was suffering from shock, he poured her a cup of tea that he had made just five minutes earlier, spooning plenty of sugar into it.

When the ambulance and police arrived, Matthew went down to the lower gardens with them while Sharon stayed in his house with a policewoman who was getting details from her. When the ambulance crew examined Celia they could find no signs of life and although Matthew had been told to stay a couple of steps back, he could see Celia's face and saw how serene she looked, a tiny smile on her face and Matthew was thankful that although she was alone when she died, she was not in distress.

On Monday at the youth club, the teenagers were all talking in low voices about Celia being found dead in the gardens early on Sunday morning and they reckoned that she had seen the ghost and as she was 'an elderly person' the shock had killed her. They vowed that they would NEVER go into the gardens on an evening, an opinion that was shared by the boys as well as the girls.

Matthew had listened to various people – a lot of them came to his door to 'see how he was' but mainly to get the story from him as Sharon Buckle had taken herself off to her sister's house at Whitby just to get away from what had happened. He soon realised that he was the only one that knew that the 'ghost' was Celia's own invented apparition but that almost everyone now believed the ghost was real and that actually seeing it had been the cause of Celia's demise.

The police had asked Matthew if he knew whether Celia had intended to meet anyone that evening as there were two cups with the flask in her bag and a packet of biscuits. Matthew had an inkling that Celia may have taken the flask and two cups just in case he had walked down to the gardens as he had on the Thursday evening and they could have shared the flask. The thought distressed him a great deal because if he *had* walked down to the gardens, he would have been there when she was stricken and perhaps he could have done something to save her. When he related this to D.I. Spence who had asked the question, the detective told him that usually in cases like this Matthew wouldn't have been able to save Celia - even if a doctor had been standing next to her he wouldn't have been able to save her either. He told him his own father had died in similar circumstances and he'd been told this by his own doctor when he'd admitted having the same feelings that Matthew had expressed to him. This brought Matthew a great deal of comfort but he still felt somehow that he had let Celia down.

That evening as he sat in his armchair he thought sadly about Celia's death – she was only sixty-six and until the coroner's verdict was released the presumption was that she had suffered an aneurysm, but Matthew took solace in the expression he had seen on Celia's face, almost as if there had been a glimpse of paradise just beforehand. There had been no sign of pain or suffering, she had looked contented.

Ah, Celia, he thought sadly, *at least you did it, you got the message across. They believed you. They won't be going into the gardens again and causing mischief. It's just a pity that you had to sacrifice your life for it.*

*****

www.ingramcontent.com/pod-product-compliance
Lightning Source LLC
Chambersburg PA
CBHW051949150726
47999CB00004B/1311